A Candlelight Ecstasy Romance

"YOU'RE GIVING ME DOUBLE MESSAGES," SONNY SAID GRIMLY.

"Which do you want me to believe, Lissa? Your words when you tell me you don't want to be involved, or the way you respond when I touch you?"

"Sonny, I admit that when you kiss me I go a little crazy. But there are reasons . . ." She caught herself and looked away guiltily.

"I'd like to hear those reasons," he said quietly. "I'd like to know what's more important than what happens when we touch."

"I can't explain!"

"Lissa . . . is there someone else?"

"No!" she burst out, much too quickly to sound convincing. Sonny sat back and looked at her in silence. Lissa knew she had hurt him. But surely it was better if Sonny thought there was another man in her life. Then he would never need to know the *true* secret she was keeping . . .

CANDLELIGHT ECSTASY CLASSIC ROMANCES

THE TEMPESTUOUS LOVERS,
Suzanne Simmons

SWEET EMBER,
Bonnie Drake

OCEAN OF REGRETS,
Noelle Berry McCue

RIGHT OF POSSESSION,
Jayne Castle

CANDLELIGHT ECSTASY ROMANCES®

504 FIRST-CLASS MALE,
Donna Kimel Vitek

505 ONCE UPON A DREAM,
JoAnn Stacey

506 MISCHIEF MAKER,
Molly Katz

507 FANCY FOOTWORK,
Cory Kenyon

508 A LOVER'S MYSTIQUE,
Eleanor Woods

509 ARIEL'S DESIRE,
Aimée Thurlo

QUANTITY SALES

Most Dell Books are available at special quantity discounts when purchased in bulk by corporations, organizations, and special-interest groups. Custom imprinting or excerpting can also be done to fit special needs. For details write: Dell Publishing Co., Inc., 1 Dag Hammarskjold Plaza, New York, NY 10017, Attn.: Special Sales Dept., or phone: (212) 605-3319.

INDIVIDUAL SALES

Are there any Dell Books you want but cannot find in your local stores? If so, you can order them directly from us. You can get any Dell book in print. Simply include the book's title, author, and ISBN number, if you have it, along with a check or money order (no cash can be accepted) for the full retail price plus 75¢ per copy to cover shipping and handling. Mail to: Dell Readers Service, Dept. FM, 6 Regent Street, Livingston, N.J. 07039.

THE VIXEN'S KISS

Jackie Black

A CANDLELIGHT ECSTASY ROMANCE®

Published by
Dell Publishing Co., Inc.
1 Dag Hammarskjold Plaza
New York, New York 10017

Copyright © 1987 by Jackie Black

All rights reserved. No part of this book may be reproduced or transmitted in any form or by any means, electronic or mechanical, including photocopying, recording or by any information storage and retrieval system, without the written permission of the Publisher, except where permitted by law.

Dell ® TM 681510, Dell Publishing Co., Inc.

Candlelight Ecstasy Romance®, 1,203,540, is a registered trademark of Dell Publishing Co., Inc., New York, New York.

ISBN: 0-440-19342-7

Printed in the United States of America

June 1987

10 9 8 7 6 5 4 3 2 1

WFH

To Our Readers:

We have been delighted with your enthusiastic response to Candlelight Ecstasy Romances®, and we thank you for the interest you have shown in this exciting series.

In the upcoming months we will continue to present the distinctive sensuous love stories you have come to expect only from Ecstasy. We look forward to bringing you many more books from your favorite authors and also the very finest work from new authors of contemporary romantic fiction.

As always, we are striving to present the unique, absorbing love stories that you enjoy most—books that are more than ordinary romance. Your suggestions and comments are always welcome. Please write to us at the address below.

Sincerely,

The Editors
Candlelight Romances
1 Dag Hammarskjold Plaza
New York, New York 10017

THE VIXEN'S KISS

CHAPTER ONE

Amid the usual cacophony backstage, Elizabeth Farrell sat in front of a cracked mirror carefully smoothing white makeup over her face while she mentally went over a catechism of chemical formulas she was determined not to let slip from her memory.

"Five minutes, Lissa!" Jay Baker reminded her as he reached behind her to grab a purple feather boa she'd promised him he could borrow for that evening's show.

Elizabeth nodded absently as she picked up a black eyeliner pencil and began to outline her huge violet eyes in a bold, garish design that Jay paused a second behind her to admire in the mirror.

"Far *out!*" he said with a grin. "What color wig are you going to wear with that getup you've got on?"

"The orange one," Elizabeth answered, frowning slightly at having to break her concentration in order to answer the irrepressible Jay.

"Exquisite!" Jay brought his long, graceful fingers, the nails of which were longer than Elizabeth's and painted purple to match the boa he'd borrowed, to his mouth and kissed the tips of them before flinging the imaginary caress in Elizabeth's direction. "You'll knock 'em dead!"

"Uh-huh," Elizabeth again answered absently, and as Jay glided away, she resumed her mental exercises while she deftly finished applying the makeup which concealed her delicate, patrician features from the crowds of people who attended the Freaky Foursome concerts.

Finished with a minute to spare, Elizabeth stood up and gave her outlandish costume a last glance in the mirror before she grabbed up her tambourine and hurried to join the other three members of the Freaky Foursome—her brother, Danny, and his two lifelong friends, Jay Baker and Jerry Madison—at the entrance to the stage.

Danny turned and inspected his sister with a frown. "You're cutting it too close, sis," he whispered hurriedly, barely audible to Elizabeth over the introductory remarks of the show's host. "I know this is a charity gig, but that's no excuse."

Elizabeth gave her brother a level look, reminding him silently that the only reason she was there at all was to help him out, that she'd been helping him out for almost a year now, which was far longer than she'd ever intended to replace his lead singer, and that she was becoming increasingly impatient to go to medical school rather than make a spectacle of herself onstage for her brother's benefit.

Danny had the grace to look a little sheepish as he shrugged and whispered, "Soon, sis . . . soon. I'm auditioning prospects tomorrow."

Elizabeth was beginning to have grave doubts about Danny's promises to audition female singers to take her place. Why was it her brother never permitted anyone else to be present at these so-called auditions he said he held? True, he was the leader of the group, and as such, he was entitled to pick the other members. But it seemed to Elizabeth it would have been helpful—and perhaps a great deal faster —to have the opinions of the rest of the Foursome.

There was no time to dwell on her doubts, however, as the local band that was backing them up that night began to play an introduction and Danny pulled her onstage to the accompaniment of swelling applause.

Automatically, Elizabeth fell into her role and began the skipping, slinking gyrations that went with the music while she rattled her tambourine in time with the heavy beat. Danny ran to the keyboard, Jay twirled himself completely around and around, making the purple feather boa he'd borrowed from Elizabeth swirl dramatically with his movements while he stroked his bass guitar for all it was worth, and Jerry seated himself behind the drums and began the intricate backup rhythm that made almost everyone in the auditorium want to dance.

Dr. Fenwick (Sonny) Strotherton III was one of the exceptions. It wasn't only his personal aesthetics that were appalled by the costumes and behavior of the four performers on the stage who were producing a sound that jarred his nerves and his ears. It was the influence the group had on his twelve-year-old daughter, Maggie, that really disturbed him.

Sonny took his duty as his little girl's sole parent extremely seriously, and he had worried during the two years since he'd lost his wife as a result of an automobile accident that he couldn't raise Maggie alone as well as he wanted to. There were so many other influences on children these days, after all . . . such as groups like the Freaky Foursome.

His worries escalated as Maggie grabbed his arm with one hand and pointed at the female member of the group onstage with the other.

"Look, Daddy, look!" she shrieked. "That's the Vixen! Isn't she fantastic?!"

Sonny allowed his morose gaze to rest on the woman his daughter admired so much and concealed a wince. Since they were seated only a few rows back from the stage, and his eyesight was excellent, he had no trouble seeing the garish white face decorated with slashes of orange lipstick and rouge, the eyes that were so boldly accented in black makeup that they seemed to leap out at one, and the spiky orange hair that looked as though it had been styled by a food processor.

Sonny let his eyes travel lower and concealed another wince as he took in the costume the Vixen wore. She had on a black top that would have done a prostitute proud, a *very* short orange-and-black-striped satin skirt, black patterned hose, black high-heeled shoes, and she wore a vivid yellow feather boa around her neck which trailed down her back almost to her ankles. Sonny wasn't even aware that the figure the costume adorned was excellent. He was too put off by the exterior to notice.

All in all, the woman was a mess as far as Sonny was concerned, but to his daughter, Maggie, the Vixen obviously was a role model to be admired and emulated. He'd had to threaten his child with the loss of everything she held dear in life in order to persuade her to dress decently and wash out the orange streak she'd painted in her hair before coming to this concert. And if the concert hadn't been a fundraiser for the new electron microscope his hospital needed desperately, Sonny wouldn't have consented to come at all, much less bring his daughter. But Maggie had threatened him with everything *he* held dear in life if he didn't bring her along, and Sonny, telling himself he needed to be broadminded and try to become more tolerant of what appealed to his daughter, had given in.

He regretted it now. While Maggie bounced up and down in her seat in time to the music, Sonny ground his teeth, stared at his daughter's new role model with loathing, wondered for the millionth time why his child had to be so hard to raise, and prayed for a quick end to this miserable excuse for a concert. As far as he could remember, he hadn't made life so difficult for his own parents.

The first song ended, and the spotlight moved to Danny behind the keyboard. Grinning widely, he grabbed up a guitar and joined Lissa and Jay center stage.

"Thank you . . . thank you, everyone." Danny spoke into the microphone, his grin showing his beautiful white teeth. He wore a wide red sweatband around his head to hold back his long, thick black hair, and his costume, while more sedate than Elizabeth's or Jay's, was still slightly offbeat. He had on a black T-shirt, a white linen Italian-style jacket, black leather pants, and white loafers without socks.

"Some of the nonmedical people in this crowd may be wondering why a group such as the Freaky Foursome is doing a benefit for a hospital," Danny continued, and a ripple of laughter echoed from the audience.

Elizabeth, however, immediately grew anxious, hoping her brother wasn't going to say anything that might reveal to the audience who she was. She had worked hard to maintain her personal anonymity while helping her brother out. It was hard enough for a female to be taken seriously in the medical community without having it become known that she was the famous Vixen of the Freaky Foursome.

Sonny wasn't listening to the young man at the microphone. He was sunk in gloom over the way Maggie's eyes never left the Vixen.

"But those of you who know that my father was a physician here in Boston understand my group's desire to help the hospital get the electron microscope it needs," Danny continued, glancing blandly at Elizabeth, who immediately let out her breath with relief, because Danny had said *my* father rather than *our* father.

There was a raucous cheer from the tuxedoed men and elaborately gowned women in the audience, as well as from their young, well-bred offspring, and Elizabeth smiled, pleased by the reaction.

Her attention was caught briefly by the contrasting expression of one man in the audience, however. Though he was very attractive, his features were twisted into a scowl and he hadn't cheered with the rest of the people. Elizabeth was disagreeably amused. Here was one man who didn't seem to appreciate the Freaky Foursome's charity. But perhaps he wasn't a physician, which might explain his lack of enthusiasm.

The young girl beside him, however, was looking at Elizabeth with an enthralled expression, and Elizabeth automatically gave the girl an especially warm smile, which made the youngster open her mouth in ecstatic shock that her heroine had actually noticed her and smiled at her!

"Anyway," Danny went on as Elizabeth saw the young girl tug at the hostile man's sleeve and speak urgently to him, which only made his scowl turn into an outright glare, "we're here, and we hope you made all the money you need from ticket sales. Now the Vixen will sing 'You're the Only Man for Me,' the song that's climbing the charts these days."

With an inner sigh of resignation, and a brief sense of regret that her talent for singing was interfering with the rest of her life, Elizabeth stepped to the microphone and swayed while the band and the other members of the Foursome played an introduction.

Then, starting in a low, sexy voice that would rise up and down the scale with effortless ease during the course of the song, Elizabeth husked the opening words into the microphone: "I lie awake all night remembering . . . my heart and body find no peace or ease. I want a man who loved me once with everything . . . then left me lonely when I somehow failed to please."

Without in the least planning it, Elizabeth's gaze became snared with that of the man who had been glaring at her earlier as she half-sang, half-spoke the next words . . .

"Oh, Lord, what do I do . . . how do I make him see . . . that he's the only man for me . . . the *only* man for me."

As she quickly turned her eyes away from the man's handsome face and continued the song scanning the rest of the audience, Elizabeth couldn't help feeling pleased that he had stopped glaring and was now looking both puzzled and moved by her performance. She supposed he hadn't thought a group like the Freaky Foursome could make good music. And though making good music was not really her goal in life, she was human enough to feel good about having dented the man's preconceptions.

The concert was long, and despite the fact that the group wasn't getting paid for it, they gave their best and were gratified by the reception they received from the dignified audience. They knew there had been a lot of controversy about asking them to perform this benefit—some of the more staid members of the medical community would have preferred a symphony. But the fundraising wisdom of the young manager of the hospital's development office had prevailed, and he was having his judgment borne out as the audience thoroughly enjoyed the entertainment.

After their last number, and three curtain calls, Elizabeth was exhausted. She was grateful that there would be a three-day hiatus before the group had to be in New York for a recording session. That would give her a good night's sleep in her own bed, then time for some uninterrupted study of her father's medical books and journals.

Unaware that the man and his young daughter she had noticed in the audience were starting a monumental argument over her, Elizabeth slipped backstage, where she and the rest of the group spent the next fifteen minutes receiving congratulations.

Usually, by now, Elizabeth would have wiped off all traces of her makeup, changed clothes to something light-years away from the style of her costume, donned concealing dark glasses and a scarf and been working her way unobtrusively through the crowd backstage to the exit. It helped that she didn't have to carry anything with her. One of the guys always took care of the tambourine and costumes so that there was nothing she had to carry that would identify her as a member of the Freaky Foursome.

But she was trapped tonight, and she endured the avid stares of the civilians with good humor, grateful that none of them was anyone who had known her father or her and Danny. Just when she thought it was ending, however, the hostile man and his daughter showed up. And whatever the father thought of her singing, it was obvious from the way he was looking at her that he still found her makeup and costume disgusting.

"Vixen!"

It was also obvious to Elizabeth that the daughter didn't share her father's low opinion of her. The awe in her young voice when she'd called out Elizabeth's stage name was laced with sheer adoration.

Elizabeth automatically smiled at the girl, though she was made slightly uncomfortable by the child's admiration, and she made ready to do what she could to make sure her influence on the girl would be positive.

"Hello, there," she said as the girl dragged her father up to her.

"Hi," the girl responded reverently, her eyes wide and admiring as she looked Elizabeth over. Her dad was looking Elizabeth over as well, but Elizabeth saw nothing resembling admiration in his scornful ice-blue eyes.

"May I have your autograph, Vixen?" Maggie Strotherton inquired in an awed tone as she held up a little book and pencil.

Elizabeth stared down at the pretty blond girl whose eyes were the same shade as her father's and hesitated. Normally, she made it a rule never to give autographs. For one thing, she felt like a fraud since she wasn't the original Vixen. For another thing, her handwriting was abominable, just as her father's had been, which embarrassed her. And the clincher was that her handwriting was also *recognizably* abominable. Elizabeth had a superstitious fear that one day, no matter how much she tried to conceal her real identity, her handwriting would trip her up.

"Well, I don't usually give autographs . . . ," she started to say, but when the look in the young girl's eyes immediately became agonizingly disappointed, Elizabeth stifled a sigh and reached for the book and pencil.

"What's your name?" she asked the girl gently, and noticed that her gentleness was making the father frown with puzzlement again.

"Margaret Strotherton," the girl answered, her face lighting like sunshine at having Elizabeth make an exception in her rule about autographs for her. "But make it to Maggie," she added hastily. "That's what everyone calls me."

Elizabeth smiled and almost said, "They call me Lissa," but bit back the words just in time. Then she had what she considered a great idea and paused before signing the book the child had given her.

"Maggie, are you a good student?" she inquired in a serious tone.

Maggie Strotherton's expression showed her surprise at the question, as did her father's.

"I guess so," she shrugged, speaking as though it didn't matter.

Elizabeth looked at the father, raising her brows, inviting his opinion.

Sonny Strotherton noticed for the first time that if one ignored all the makeup and looked directly into the Vixen's eyes, they were a lovely shade of violet . . . and they had an intelligent expression in them as well.

"She's an excellent student when she puts her mind to it," he responded dryly, tearing his gaze from the Vixen's unexpectedly beautiful eyes to give his daughter a parental glance that clearly showed his impatience that she didn't always "put her mind to it."

Elizabeth's smile broadened and her gaze expressed humorous understanding. Catching her look, Sonny felt confused again by the conflict between her appearance and her manner.

Elizabeth returned her attention to the girl.

"Well, Maggie, I'll make an exception to my rule and give you an autograph on one condition," she said in a serious tone.

Wide-eyed, Maggie Strotherton nodded vigorously. "Anything!" she declared with adolescent fervor. "I'll do anything you say, Vixen!"

Elizabeth controlled a wince at that declaration. The effect she had on young people in her role as the Vixen was another reason she wanted out as soon as her brother could find a replacement for her.

She was always afraid that no matter how hard she tried not to be a negative influence, there was always the possibility she would be misunderstood by some young person or other, and the idea appalled her.

Elizabeth glanced at the father and saw that, predictably, he was as dismayed as she was by the amount of influence she had over his daughter.

Elizabeth considered giving the girl a lecture about emulating *anyone* too closely, then stuck to her decision to use her influence positively.

"If I give you this autograph," she said to her young admirer, "I want you to promise me that you'll try for all As at school the rest of this year."

Maggie seemed taken aback by such a request from her idol, but since the request would be relatively easy for her to grant, she nodded and shrugged, eager to please. "Sure," she said quickly. "I can do that."

Sonny Strotherton gritted his teeth at the ease with which this garishly made-up performer could gain such a promise from his stubborn daughter. He was both grateful and angry. For the barest second he wondered bitterly if his daughter would pay more attention to his instruction if he donned an outlandish costume and strummed a guitar when trying to get her to do something!

"Thank you, Maggie." Elizabeth smiled and then did her best to disguise her handwriting by writing slowly and carefully in the girl's autograph book. Naturally, she failed. It seemed no matter how hard she tried, she couldn't disguise her truly awful scrawl.

Sonny watched the laborious way Elizabeth was writing and wondered wryly if she was even literate. Maybe she was so adamant about Maggie paying attention to her schoolwork because she'd had no education herself and regretted it. His animosity toward the Vixen softened slightly, angling toward pity.

Finished, Elizabeth handed the pencil and book back to their owner, then lightly touched the girl's shining blond hair with gentle fingers, thinking the child was truly lovely. Glancing at the father again, she decided it wasn't surprising the girl was so pretty when her father was such a stunningly handsome man.

"I've got to go," she said lightly, stepping back. "Thanks for coming to the concert. I hope you enjoyed it."

Of course, Maggie didn't really have to utter the fervent affirmation that she had loved every second of the concert. It was obvious. The father, too, Elizabeth thought wryly, had enjoyed it more than he would ever admit, and acting with a perverse need to disconcert him, she gave him a sexy wink. She almost laughed outright when her action brought an immediate expression of stiff disapproval to his distinctive face.

Elizabeth gave the two of them a little farewell wave, then turned her back and strode in her normal graceful style toward the dressing room where she would wipe off her makeup and change clothes.

As Elizabeth walked away, Maggie slipped her hand into her father's and stared avidly after her.

"Oh, Daddy," she sighed in a starstruck voice, "isn't she wonderful?"

Sonny cut off an automatic denial just in time before he answered in a way that would start another fight between him and his daughter. Instead, he said nothing at all, and his ice-blue eyes were thoughtful as he watched the woman who had slithered all over the stage in such a provocative way earlier, walk away in an entirely different fashion. With her head up and back straight, she seemed suddenly to take on an aura of dignity, and he found himself realizing that underneath her godawful clothes she had a delectable figure.

"Well, Daddy, she is, isn't she?!" Maggie persisted, and as Sonny looked down into his daughter's pretty face and saw the beginnings of a storm rising behind her clear blue eyes, he stifled an inner sigh and forced himself to reply, though his true feelings were ambivalent at best.

"Well, she does seem to know the value of a good education," he said aloud, thinking silently, *even though she doesn't seem to have had one herself.*

"Oh, pooh!" Maggie snorted, dragging her hand out of her father's. "She probably just asked me to make good grades 'cause you were with me."

Sonny raised a very male eyebrow as he considered his daughter's conclusion.

"No," he finally shook his head, surprised to find that he meant what he was about to say. "I don't think that young woman would say something she didn't mean to a girl your age." He frowned over the contradictory impressions he'd gotten of the lead singer of the Freaky Foursome.

"Well, I'm going to keep my promise to her." Maggie sniffed. "I guess that ought to make you happy we came to the concert even though you didn't want to bring me."

"Yes." Sonny nodded, steering his daughter toward the exit. "That makes me very happy."

As his daughter smiled smugly over the victory she presumed she'd won over her father, Sonny reflected uneasily that he had also been strangely happy for a brief instant when the freakily dressed Vixen had started singing that song about "You're the only man for me" and had looked right at him while she said the words.

You definitely need a vacation, old man, he told himself dryly as he escorted Maggie outside the auditorium. *Preferably one where you leave Maggie at home and go to a Caribbean island infested with beautiful women who would like nothing better than to show you a good time. Either you've been working too hard or you're losing your mind when you can get excited by a silly song sung by a nut dressed up like a tramp whom your own daughter views as the next best thing to a goddess in the land of the weird.*

As Elizabeth drifted toward sleep that night, safe in the snug bed that had been hers since childhood, her thoughts turned idly toward the man with the unusual, and beautiful, blue eyes who couldn't make up his mind whether she was worthy of approval or should be condemned as a detriment to society, but who definitely disapproved of his daughter's infatuation with her. What was he doing at the concert when the Freaky Foursome was obviously not to his taste? Was he some businessman who found it expedient to support hospital charities, or had his daughter simply dragooned him into coming?

What does it matter?, she thought sleepily as she snuggled down further in her bed. *You'll never see him again, and if you did, what would be the point? He's not the type to become interested in a rock singer, and you haven't got time for a private life now anyway.*

She intended to stop thinking about him and go to sleep, but just as she thought she'd succeeded, another question intruded into her consciousness. Was the man married . . . or was he divorced or widowed and therefore single and available?

Frowning, she shook her head, wondering why the man persisted in staying on her mind. Besides all the obvious reasons why she shouldn't be thinking about him at all, the only thing about him that had appealed to her was his looks. She'd never been attracted to stuffed shirts, and though the man was exceedingly handsome, well-built, and possessed the most gorgeous blue eyes she'd ever seen, he was definitely a stuffed shirt. He would probably be a dead bore on a date.

Smiling over her conclusion, Elizabeth promptly fell asleep, and her first thought upon awakening late the next morning had to do with insisting that Danny let her sit in on those auditions he had said he would be conducting that day. She was tired of putting off her own life to accommodate his. There must be a female singer somewhere who could take her place without anyone being the wiser.

I'm not delaying medical school much longer, and that's all there is to it, she thought determinedly as she brushed her teeth. *It's time for Danny to face the fact that my needs deserve as much consideration as he's always believed his do.*

CHAPTER TWO

Downstairs at the breakfast table in the cheerful nook fronted by bay windows, Elizabeth found Jay, clad in a white karate-type robe, drinking coffee and reading the financial page of the morning paper.

"Morning." Elizabeth nodded at him as she went to the counter to pour herself some coffee. Jay grunted a response without looking up. When she joined him at the table a moment later, he was muttering to himself in a displeased way that alerted Elizabeth as to what was on his mind.

"Stocks down?" she inquired sympathetically.

"Not all of them," Jay growled. "Just the new one I bought a week ago."

Elizabeth hid a smile. Jay played the stock market with the fervor of a gambling addict and nothing could depress his normal cheerfulness like a loss. He seemed to take it personally when a stock he chose didn't perform as expected—as though it were a reflection on him.

"But I'm sure it's only temporary," he added, sounding more optimistic now. "The president of the company died of a heart attack unexpectedly and until they've replaced him, the stock will probably slide a bit."

"How thoughtless of him," Elizabeth said dryly.

Alerted by her tone, Jay lowered his paper and grinned at her. "Yes, wasn't it," he teased. "In future, I guess I'll have to check out the health of a company's management before I invest."

Elizabeth made a face and sipped her coffee, then asked, "Where's Danny? Still sleeping?"

Jay's face immediately assumed an expression of smooth innocence that made Elizabeth suspicious.

"Why, I believe he's already left to do those auditions he set up," he replied in a vague tone. Then he dove behind his paper, increasing Elizabeth's suspicions.

"I wanted to go with him," she said casually, concealing the grimness she was feeling. There was no response from Jay. "Where is he holding the auditions, did he say?" she asked, still in a casual way. "Maybe I could drop in there later."

"Ummm . . . I don't believe he mentioned where he was going to do it," Jay mumbled, sounding distracted.

Elizabeth sat for a moment staring at an announcement on the front page that unemployment had gone up 0.1 percent in the last quarter.

"Jay," she said quietly, and at getting no response, she reached across the table and jerked the paper from in front of Jay's face. He looked both startled and offended as he tried to hang on to it. "Jay, it couldn't be that my beloved brother has no intention of replacing me, could it?" she demanded in a threatening manner, dropping all pretense of casualness now.

Jay frowned and looked annoyed. "For heaven's sakes," he said petulantly, jerking the paper out of Elizabeth's hand. "He's told you he's trying, hasn't he? Don't you trust your own brother?"

"Not entirely," Elizabeth said in a grim voice. "He . . . and *you* —" she added at remembering the truth of what she was going to say, "—have wanted the sort of success the group is enjoying now all your lives. And it's not beyond the realm of possibility that you've convinced yourselves it won't last if I go. Which is ridiculous," she said with firm conviction. "Any female singer can dress up like a clown and cavort onstage as convincingly as I do."

Jay slowly lowered his paper, the look in his normally merry brown eyes turning shrewd.

"You think that's all there is to it?" he inquired dryly.

Elizabeth looked away. She suspected what argument he was going to use on her next, but before she could think of some way to rebut it, he was already on the attack.

"What about your singing?" he demanded. "Even if you didn't have an excellent, and more importantly, *memorable,* solo voice, it isn't that easy to find someone who can blend in on the duets with Danny. You know what an unusual tone he has."

"Meredith could," Elizabeth reminded him of the original Vixen.

Jay grimaced. "She could sing the duets, yes," he agreed, "but her solos didn't grab anybody the way yours do, even if she'd been mature enough to put her career first and Danny second."

Elizabeth sighed, but not in defeat. She was determined to resist the pressure Jay was exerting to convince her the Freaky Foursome would collapse if she didn't remain a member of it.

"Jay, there's someone somewhere who can take my place," she said firmly, "but if Danny doesn't even look, we'll never find her. Now is he really holding auditions today or is he off with some groupie having a little intimate recreation while he conveniently forgets that I have a life of my own I want to get back to?"

Jay looked pained. "Danny doesn't date groupies," he reminded her on a long-suffering sigh.

"No, that's right," Elizabeth responded sarcastically. "He's got enough admirers here in the old hometown whom he knows personally to make that unnecessary."

"All I know is what he tells me," Jay said with blithe unconcern as he headed toward the door of the kitchen. "And as much as I'd like to stay and rap with you about it, I'm due for a session with my karate instructor, so I have to go."

"How convenient!" Elizabeth snapped.

Jay paused to face her, the expression on his face dripping with surprised hurt, which didn't fool Elizabeth for a second. Jay was a master at such games, but she'd known him too long to fall for them anymore.

"My dear, I *am* entitled to a certain amount of relaxation between engagements, am I not?" he huffed. "You'll bury yourself in those stuffy medical books, which for some unknown reason *you* regard as relaxing, and Jerry is with his family going gaga over his newest heir, so why must I let your paranoia deprive me of my own amusements?"

"Oh, get lost!" Elizabeth grated, surging to her feet to replenish her coffee. "I'd rather take a beating than listen to one of your acts about how underprivileged you are right now!"

"Very well," Jay responded with dignity as he pivoted and left the room.

Later on that day after Jay had finished his karate lesson and Danny had finished entertaining a young woman he had known for several years, they discussed Lissa's suspicions.

"You were right," Jay said as he got his bass guitar out of its case in preparation for working on a song Danny was writing for their new album. "Lissa did plan to horn in on your fictitious auditions today. It's a good thing you got out of the house early."

Danny grunted as he leaned forward over the piano keys and marked a note on a sheet of music. "I always know what she's thinking," he said absently as he played a chord, tilting his head as though to hear better, which made his thick dark hair fall forward over his wide brow.

"Well, since that's true," Jay responded, his tone wry, "you must be aware that she won't be put off much longer." He sighed, shaking his head. "What a disgusting development. We worked our butts off for years to make it, but it wasn't until you got her to help us out when Meredith left that we made it big. And she's convinced it wasn't due to her! She thinks we can replace her just like that!"

Jay snapped his fingers, then spotted a tiny fleck of purple that he'd missed with the polish remover that morning and promptly put the nail in his mouth to scrape the fleck off with his teeth.

"I'll handle it," Danny said absently, his mind more on the song he was picking out on the piano than his sister's desires.

"How?" Jay demanded around his fingernail. "I'm telling you, she's about to bolt!" He looked a little guilty then, and added, "And I guess I really can't blame her. She wants to be a doctor as badly as we want to be successful musicians."

Danny looked up with a frown, tired of Jay's worries about Elizabeth. "I can stall her for another six months," he said irritably, "and by that time, we'll be so big we can pick and choose anyone we want to replace Lissa. It won't cost her anything but a little time. Uncle Ferris has her spot in medical school sewn up, so it's not as if she has to worry she'll lose it. Now stop worrying, Jay, and listen to this. I think I've got it fixed."

Jay shrugged and moved closer, his attention focusing on the tune Danny was playing, his right hand moving automatically to the strings of his bass as he began to join in.

Back at the house, Elizabeth was standing in Jay's room beside the middle-aged woman who had worked for the Farrells for as long as she could remember, shaking her head over the mess Jay had left to be cleaned up.

"He's worse than a tornado," Maude Stanley voiced Elizabeth's own sentiments. "Makes me wish he'd get a place of his own every time you all come home. Why doesn't he, honey? Ain't he makin' enough money to pay his own way?"

Elizabeth sighed and shrugged. "Yes, but I can't decide whether he likes to stay with us because he hasn't any family of his own now and regards us as the next best thing, or whether he just wants that much more to invest in the stock market."

"Don't he want no social life?" Maude asked archly.

Elizabeth glanced at Maude, aware that the woman had her suspicions about Jay because of his certain effeminate characteristics and because he never dated. Elizabeth herself had long since given up trying to figure out what Jay's inclinations were. He was such a paradox, it was impossible to reach a conclusion.

She shrugged again, ignoring the question. "Just do the best you can, Maude," she said, patting the older woman on the shoulder as she determined silently that she would start adding a little bonus to Maude's pay when she and Danny and Jay were home. Maude wasn't getting any younger, and it was only fair to pay her extra when there was extra work to do.

"I ain't promisin' nothin'," Maude said tartly as she bent to start picking up the clothing Jay had strung all over the room, "except that this place will look a *little* better when I get done than it does now. Not that it'll last past five minutes when he gets back and starts in on it again."

Elizabeth smiled and left Jay's room to go to her father's library to study for a while. As she entered the paneled room with its book-lined walls, she felt a pang of loneliness for a second, wishing as she always did at coming in here that she would find her father sitting behind his desk as usual, ready to talk to her about one of his cases. She wondered how long it was going to take before she got over missing her dad so much. He'd been dead for almost two years now, and while the pain wasn't quite as sharp as it had been in the beginning, it was still hard to accept that she would never see him again.

She had kept up Daniel Farrell's subscription to *The New England Journal of Medicine,* and now she decided to catch up on what she'd missed while the Freaky Foursome had been on tour rather than read one of the medical tomes of her father's she normally studied.

By the time she surfaced again several hours later and stood to stretch the kinks out of her body, it was dinnertime, and Elizabeth looked forward to hearing whether Danny had made any progress on his auditions that day. But when she entered the kitchen, she found only a casserole Maude had prepared along with a note explaining that Danny had called saying he and Jay wouldn't be home for dinner.

"Damn!" she muttered, flinging the note aside before placing her hands on her slender hips in an attitude of disgust. "Danny Farrell, I don't trust you one little bit anymore," she voiced her thoughts with narrowed eyes. "I'll bet the family silver you no more auditioned any singers today than I did!"

But having voiced her conclusion aloud, Elizabeth was struck by an idea it aroused. If Danny wasn't going to look for a replacement for her, why couldn't she do it herself? A few ads in the trade papers . . . discreet ones, of course . . . a few secret hours when she could get away for interviews . . . why not?

And feeling excited by the idea, Elizabeth slipped the casserole in the oven, then sat down at the kitchen table to begin drafting an ad for a singer who had just the right voice, and was just the right size, to fool anyone into thinking she was the past, present, and future Vixen. Of course, she wouldn't tell any candidates exactly what they were auditioning for until she was satisfied they could do it, and would be willing to keep their mouths shut in exchange for the chance to make it big on the rock scene.

By the time Elizabeth went to bed that night, Danny and Jay hadn't come home. But Elizabeth was decidedly optimistic that she would eventually foil her brother's plan to keep her chained to the Freaky Foursome for the rest of her natural life. She could be as sneaky as Danny when circumstances called for it, and she was certainly as determined to lead her own life as Danny was to co-opt it.

Sometime later, Danny and Jay cruised slowly by the Farrell home with Danny at the wheel of his brand new black Mondial Ferrari.

"The lights are out. Looks like she's gone to bed," Jay said over a big yawn. "Come on . . . park it, Danny. I'm ready for some sleep."

"Yeah, me, too." Danny nodded as he made a quick U-turn and pulled into the driveway of his family home. "Especially since I'm going to have to get up early again tomorrow and get out of the house before she wakes up and wants to know if I found anyone today."

Jay chuckled. "This could be hard on your health," he joked.

"Nah." Danny shrugged. "I'll just go down to the studio and sack out on the couch for a couple of hours before I start work."

"Start work on what?" Jay asked as he and Danny got out of the car and started for the back door. "Everything's all set for the album now, isn't it?"

"Yeah, but I always like to have a little something in reserve," Danny replied, his expression serious. "You never know when you're going to need it."

"Hell," Jay scoffed in a whisper as Danny opened the back door as quietly as possible. "You're just a workaholic, Danny. You couldn't stop writing songs if you had a million of them in reserve."

Danny just smiled, and the two of them tiptoed upstairs to their rooms, exchanging a whispered good night on the landing before each disappeared to get as much sleep as possible before Elizabeth woke up and got on the warpath.

Several blocks away, Sonny Strotherton, feeling like an adolescent idiot on the prowl, checked to make sure his daughter was securely asleep before he slipped down to the family den, retrieved a record album he had bought on impulse that day from where he'd hidden it, donned the stereo headphones, and settled back to prove to himself that the song the Vixen had sung at the concert the night before was just another song . . . that there was nothing special about it.

Half an hour later, he went to bed feeling half-angry, half-bewildered that one voice out of thousands, singing words that were really pretty mundane love song stuff, could reach right down into his gut and create havoc.

I'm telling you, you need a vacation, he told himself as he slammed a fist into his pillow, feeling grimly resentful that he had given in to the urge to buy the album that was now safely hidden away again. *Either that or one of these days you're going to start accepting some of those invitations the nurses practically print on their foreheads whenever they see you coming, and you've got a rule about that, remember?*

As he stared at the dark ceiling over his head hoping the hunger in his body which the Vixen's song had aroused would quiet down soon so he could get some sleep, Sonny wished wholeheartedly, and not for the first time, that he wasn't in the situation in which he found himself.

After his wife's death, when he'd finally started dating again, he had quickly found out that he couldn't date any woman more than twice before Maggie found some way to sabotage the romance. So far, he'd let her get away with it because it just so happened that he hadn't found anyone he wanted to date more than twice. When he did, he planned to get around Maggie somehow. He'd figure out how when he needed to. And because of his own rigid ideas about relationships in the workplace, he had stayed clear of any involvements with nurses, though without being unduly egotistical, he was positive he was considered the biggest catch on the market.

Meanwhile, however, he was left with no outlet for his very normal, increasingly urgent male needs, and he considered his long-term celibacy was at the root of his highly unusual reaction to his daughter's heroine, the Vixen . . . or rather to that dumb song she sang so convincingly. Trampy-looking rock stars just weren't his style . . . never had been, even in his younger days. So how else explain why he had gone out and bought that silly album, sneaked around like a fugitive to play it, and sat there becoming increasingly aroused while he listened to it?

I'll see if I can arrange my schedule to take off a week next month, he thought as he began to grow sleepy at last. *It'll be cold and nasty here by then, and a trip to a Club Med somewhere will be just the thing to ease my problems for a while. I can sample charms all day long and all night long if I want to, then walk away with no complications to worry about.*

It was only an instant before he fell asleep that he wondered why the thought of no complications left him feeling lonelier than ever. Fortunately, he was too tired to dwell on the question, and the next morning, as usual, he had too many other things on his mind to think about his emotional well-being . . . or lack of it.

CHAPTER THREE

On the last day of taping their album in New York, Lissa was grateful that everything went smoothly and they were able to finish early. That would give her a few hours to audition singers in the small studio she'd rented before she had to appear with the Foursome at a nightclub that night.

As Lissa put on her coat and gloves, she was amused by how quickly Danny disappeared out of sight so that she couldn't tackle him about the auditions *he* was supposed to be holding. She was positive now that Danny had no intention of finding anyone to replace her, but she went through the motions of prodding him about it so that he wouldn't suspect she'd taken things into her own hands.

Half an hour later, Lissa strode into the anteroom of the studio she was using and was pleased to find half a dozen women waiting for her.

"Hello." She nodded and smiled at the applicants, her eyes scanning them quickly in an effort to discard those who were obviously unsuitable. She didn't have a lot of time to waste, and there was no sense sitting through auditions with singers who were either too small or too large to fool anyone that they were the Vixen.

"I'm Mary Hope," Lissa introduced herself, using the fictitious name she had picked in a spirit of ironic humor to conceal her real identity. She was beginning to think she should have picked "Nary a Hope," since she had already auditioned over a hundred singers and as yet hadn't found even a single one who fit her requirements.

There was a murmur of greeting from the varied group, who were all eyeing her with expressions of hope of their own.

"I'm sorry," Lissa said as she drew off her gloves and stuffed them in the side pocket of her purse, "but there are certain physical requirements for this job as well as singing talent, and I'm afraid you and you—" she pointed to two of the women, "don't fit the bill."

Immediately, the expressions of the two women who were being discarded before they ever had a chance to sing showed first disappointment, then belligerence.

"What is this gig?" one of them said with sneering anger. "A little private party where we're expected to do more than sing?"

Lissa understood the woman's disappointment, as well as the attempt she was making to put doubts into the minds of the other applicants.

"I assure you," she said, reaching into her purse to withdraw some money, "this job is nothing like that. Here," she added, offering each of the two women she'd rejected out of hand enough money for cab fare. "I know you're disappointed, so let me pay your transportation at least."

One of the women took the money gratefully, though she still looked disappointed, but the one who'd spoken merely curled her lip, grabbed her coat, and stomped out the door.

When the two were gone, Lissa turned to the other four, noting that a couple of them had become disturbed by the possibility that the outspoken rejectee might have been right about the nature of the job.

"The job really isn't anything at all as she suggested," Lissa said with convincing sincerity, and was gratified when most of the doubts seemed to disappear.

"So why do we have to have a certain look?" one of the remaining women asked curiously, however.

"I can't explain that until I've determined whether any of you has the right voice for the job," Lissa said, a slight apology in her voice. "Now," she continued as she shrugged out of her coat and opened the door to the studio which contained a piano. "May I see you one at a time?"

The woman nearest the studio door quickly stood up and followed

Lissa inside where Lissa tossed her coat over a chair before seating herself at the piano.

"Do you know this one?" she asked, playing a few bars of "You're the Only Man for Me."

"Sure." The woman shrugged as she came to lean against the piano.

It took no more than a minute for Lissa to know that the woman's voice was entirely wrong, but while she would have preferred to end the audition then and there, her innate courtesy made her allow the singer to finish the song.

"How'd I do?" Lissa was asked when she stood up from the piano.

Lissa hated these continual rejections she had to dole out, both from the standpoint that she was frustrated on her own behalf, and because she sympathized with the rejectees. However, there was no point in giving false hope to anyone, so she performed her task as gently as possible.

"You have a lovely voice," she said sincerely as she directed the singer to the door, "but I'm afraid it just isn't right for this particular job." And as the woman's face reflected her disappointment, Lissa handed her cabfare as she'd done for the first two applicants. Though she knew it wasn't necessary, it made her feel better about having to turn people down.

It didn't take long to reject the next two women either, and Lissa was feeling depressed by the time the last applicant joined her in the studio.

"Darla Simmons," the woman introduced herself informally as she set her coat and purse aside.

"It's nice to meet you, Darla," Lissa replied, her mood lightening somewhat as she eyed the other woman. At least this one was exactly the right size, and even her eyes were a similar color to Lissa's. The difference in hair color and complexion—Darla was a blonde—didn't matter since Lissa had never appeared on stage without a wig and heavy, concealing makeup. Now if Darla could only sing . . .

"You want me to do the song you've been having all the others sing?" Darla inquired, her gaze speculative, as though she was wondering why that particular song had been chosen. "I could hear through the door," she added as Lissa looked at her in surprise.

"Oh," Lissa relaxed a little. "Well, yes. If you know it . . . ?"

"Everybody knows it," Darla said with a shrug. "You can't turn on a radio without hearing it fifty times a day."

Lissa gazed at Darla curiously. "It sounds as though you don't like it," she suggested.

Darla shrugged again, a wry smile tugging at her well-shaped lips. "Oh, I like it," she said. "I'm just jealous of the Vixen's popularity, I guess." Now, she grinned, and Lissa found herself liking that grin. "It may sound egotistical," she admitted, "but I think I'm as good as the Vixen, and I sure dress better."

Lissa grinned back, liking Darla better every minute. She hated the costumes she had to wear herself, but the audience seemed to like them, and they were absolutely necessary to conceal her identity. Of course, if Darla could really sing, she would have to get over her aversion to the Vixen's style of dress, but it was too soon to even think about that yet.

Seating herself at the piano, Lissa played an introduction, and then nodded at Darla when it was time for her to come in.

Darla did so without nervousness or hesitation, and Lissa felt a little thrill of hope dart through her as the first few words rang out in the small room. Darla sang all the words rather than half-speaking them at first the way Lissa did, but there was definitely a similarity in her tone and phrasing.

Lissa let her go all the way through the song, exulting when she heard Darla sing the parts where Lissa normally sang rather than spoke herself, for Darla's voice, except for a few minor variations, was the closest to her own Lissa had yet heard.

When the song was over, Lissa tried to keep her excitement out of her voice as she said, "That was good, Darla. Now do it like the Vixen does . . . speak the first lines rather than sing them."

Again, Darla gave Lissa that speculative look that made Lissa feel uneasy. Lissa was further alarmed when Darla said, "I've got my own style, you know. I don't like to copycat."

"I understand," Lissa responded, and she did. But she also thought that if Darla were willing to compromise at first, eventually she could start interjecting that style of hers without it causing any comment. "But do it the Vixen's way for now, all right?" she requested in a casual way.

Darla shrugged. "Okay," she agreed, though she didn't sound particularly happy about it.

By the time they'd gone through the song a second time, Lissa was having to clamp down hard on her excitement. Darla's imitation of the Vixen wasn't perfect, but with a little work, Lissa thought it could be so close as not to matter. Now she needed to know if Darla's voice would blend with Danny's and if it did, Lissa faced the task of trying to ascertain if Darla would be willing to carry out the deception.

Lissa now got out a tape recorder which contained a tape of Danny singing alone.

"See if you can harmonize with this," she said, neglecting to mention who the male singer was as she played the tape through once. From the look on Darla's face, however, Lissa began to suspect that Darla knew who was on the tape, as well as actively speculating about the meaning of this whole audition.

Darla said nothing about what she was thinking, however, as she began to try to pick out the proper way to harmonize with Danny's unusual voice. This was a new song of Danny's that Lissa had taped secretly, so Darla also had to learn the words. Lissa was delighted that Darla was such a quick study when after a couple of times through the song, she finally found the proper key, had the words memorized, and belted out the song along with Danny's taped voice in a way that convinced Lissa she'd finally found her replacement . . . that is, if Darla was willing to take the job.

When the song was over, however, before Lissa could say anything, Darla fixed her with a somewhat grim stare and said, "All right . . . what's this all about? Have you got some idea of forming a group to imitate the Freaky Foursome? Because if you do, you can count me out. I don't go for that kind of piggybacking. I wouldn't like it if I were a star, and I don't think it's fair to . . ."

Darla fell silent as Lissa shook her head and held up a hand.

"That's not what I have in mind at all," Lissa said, then bit her lip as she faced the fact that she was going to have to tell Darla the truth now, which could prove dangerous if Darla turned the offer down and then spilled everything she knew to the press. Lissa knew that Danny, Jay, and Jerry would never forgive her if that happened.

Darla was eyeing Lissa suspiciously, waiting for her to continue, and Lissa took a deep breath.

"I'd like what I'm about to say to remain confidential," she started with simple honesty as she looked Darla straight in the eyes. "Would you be willing to give me your promise that you won't reveal to anyone what I'm about to tell you?"

Darla frowned, her expression puzzled. "Sure, I can promise you that," she said with blunt forthrightness, "but you'd be silly to take me at my word. In this business, promises don't always mean much."

Lissa was torn, but something about Darla's statement and attitude convinced her that Darla was different from the sort of person she was warning Lissa about.

"Maybe I am silly to trust you," she said with a shrug, "but I don't think so. You don't appear to me to have so little character. Besides," she added with a wry smile, "I have little choice. I *have* to trust you."

At that, Darla relaxed and pulled up a chair. When she was settled, she smiled at Lissa in a warmer manner. "All right," she said with a nod, "I'll keep your secret, whatever it is. It's nice to find someone in this city who isn't a complete cynic. And you've got me so curious now . . ." She grinned mischievously. ". . . that I'm about to burst. I'd promise just about anything to find out what you're doing."

Lissa smiled, then took a deep breath. "I'm the Vixen," she stated baldly, and paused to let her revelation sink in.

Darla just stared at her for a moment, at first unbelievingly, then with a searching look that Lissa knew meant she was trying to find similarities between the star she'd seen on television and this sedately dressed woman sitting in front of her.

"You're kidding," Darla said, her expression half skeptical, half convinced.

"No." Lissa shook her head and sighed. "I'm her, all right . . . not that I ever wanted to be."

Darla leaned forward, studying Lissa again. Then she leaned back, her eyes wide. "I must be crazy," she said wonderingly. "I think I believe you."

"I hope so!" Lissa said emphatically. "You're my ticket out of the limelight . . . at least I hope you are."

Now Darla looked thoroughly bewildered. "If you're telling me the truth, you're the one who's crazy!" she exclaimed. "My God, you've got it made! Why in the world would you want out?"

Lissa shut the piano lid and leaned her elbow against it, propping her head against her hand.

"It's a long story." She sighed. "Care to hear it?"

"Are you kidding?!" Darla said in an incredulous tone. "I'm *dying* to hear it. Go on . . . go on!"

Lissa knew she might be making the biggest mistake of her life, but she felt Darla was a person who could be trusted.

"Well, it's like this," she began. "Danny Farrell, the leader of the Freaky Foursome, is my brother."

"No kidding!" Darla sat wide-eyed, listening with her whole body.

"No kidding," Lissa said dryly. "I love him, but sometimes I wish he weren't my brother. He's so caught up in his music, and so single-minded about becoming a success at it, that I think he's prepared to do just about anything to have his dream."

"Seems to me like he's getting it," Darla interjected. "The Freaky Foursome is about the hottest new group on the music scene these days."

"Yes, unfortunately," Lissa replied in a mournful tone. "That's the problem. Danny and the rest of the group are convinced I'm the one responsible for their popularity. They didn't start making it big until I came on the scene, you see," she said, her impatience clear in her voice.

"Gee, that's rough," Darla responded, mocking Lissa. "It must be a real strain being so successful."

Lissa grimaced. "Oh, I know it's hard for most people to understand," she admitted. "But I never wanted to be a singer." She sounded indignant now. "I want to be a pediatrician, like my father, but I can't get away from the group and get back to school . . . at least not until there's a replacement for me," she added, fixing Darla with a purposeful look.

Darla looked stunned for a moment, then started shaking her head.

"Oh, no," she protested. "Not me."

"Why not?" Lissa persisted, practically begging Darla now. "You want to be a popular singer, don't you?"

"Sure," Darla scowled, "but I want to be me and make it my way. I don't want to sneak in the back door."

Frustrated, Lissa clenched her hands into fists and sat up straight. Then, realizing she would get nowhere by trying to browbeat Darla, she decided to explain further rather than insist.

"Look, Darla," she said forlornly, "I've already had to put off my goal a couple of times. I'd just been accepted for medical school when my dad got sick and I took off a year to be with him." Her voice was choked as she added softly, "We lost him two years ago."

Lissa saw Darla's face soften with sympathy and she quickly looked away, afraid she would start to cry if she didn't hold tight to her emotions.

"Then I had to act as dad's executrix—" she started to continue, but Darla interrupted.

"Wait a minute," she said softly. "Is Danny older or younger than you?"

"Older."

"Then why didn't your dad make him the executor?" Darla was clearly puzzled.

Lissa shook her head. "Danny didn't want it," she explained. "All he cares about is his music."

"I see," Darla said somewhat grimly, and Lissa began to be afraid that Darla was developing a prejudice against Danny.

"Danny's all right," she said quickly. "It's just that his music has always been an obsession with him. I guess he inherited his talent and dedication from our mother. Mom was a concert pianist. In fact, that's how she died . . . she was flying back in a private plane from an engagement and there was a crash."

Darla looked unconvinced about Danny, but even more sympathetic toward Lissa, which encouraged Lissa to go on.

"Anyway, about the time Dad's estate was settled, Danny's group lost its lead singer."

"Why?" Darla inquired, and Lissa wished she hadn't.

"Ah . . . she sort of fell in love with Danny," Lissa said, moving restlessly on the piano bench, "and Danny didn't feel that way about her, so she left."

"I'll bet he didn't," Darla responded in a way that made Lissa's heart sink.

"Danny couldn't help it," she defended her brother stoutly. "He's very attractive. He appeals to females of all types and ages. But he's not ready to be serious about anyone yet. As I said, all he really cares about is his music."

"Uh-huh," Darla responded in a cynical tone. "No matter what it costs anybody else, even his own sister, right?"

Lissa quickly decided to get off the subject of Danny and women.

"Well, anyway," she continued, "Danny had just gotten a decent tour lined up for the Foursome when Meredith walked out on him. He was in a real bind."

"So he appealed to you and you put what you wanted aside and helped him out." Darla sounded even more cynical now.

"I had to," Lissa said simply. "He's my brother."

"And you're his sister," Darla pointed out. "But he didn't even think about putting what he wanted aside for your benefit, did he?"

Lissa frowned, wishing she'd never gone into so much detail about what had happened. "He had the other members of the group to think about, too," she again defended Danny. "They've been together since junior high. And this was their big chance."

Darla said nothing, but Lissa didn't like the expression in her eyes.

"Listen, Darla," she said a little desperately. "I'll admit that Danny can be . . . well, somewhat *selfish* about his career. But he's also loving and talented as well. You'd like him if you got to know him . . . I'm sure of it."

Darla's look said she wasn't sure of such a thing at all.

"But even if you didn't," Lissa hastily went on, "this is a chance for you to get to the top without having to wait to be discovered."

"I've got time," Darla drawled.

"I don't," Lissa mumbled under her breath, then aloud said, "Darla, I know you want to do your own thing your own way, but don't you see that eventually you can? You might have to be my version of the Vixen at first so that no one would know there'd been a change, but gradually you can try new things . . . *your* things."

"And Danny would go along with what I wanted like a little lamb," Darla interjected with dry disbelief.

That stopped Lissa for a moment. And looking into Darla's eyes, she finally realized there was no way she was going to be able to convince her that Danny would please anyone but himself as far as what type of music the Foursome played.

Despondent, Lissa's shoulders sagged, and the trapped feeling inside her escalated.

"I wish you'd at least try it," she said, sounding hopeless.

Darla gazed at her with shrewd sympathy in her blue-violet eyes.

"Does Danny even know you're doing this?" she asked in a quiet tone.

Lissa couldn't meet Darla's eyes. "Not exactly," she muttered in a defensive way.

Darla sighed and cast her eyes at the ceiling. "In other words, he doesn't," she said with flat conviction. "What's he been doing . . . promising you he'd let you off the hook without meaning a word of it?"

Lissa winced, which gave Darla the answer she'd sought. Darla got to her feet and began pacing, while Lissa watched her in a hopeless fashion.

Finally, Darla came to a stop in front of her, and as Lissa gazed up at her face, she felt a cautious optimism begin inside her. Darla definitely looked undecided.

"I'll be honest with you," Darla finally spoke. "I've been around enough musicians like your brother to learn to hate them."

Lissa winced again, but Darla continued without a pause.

"I doubt very much that your Danny would go along with your plan even if I decide to take you up on your offer. And," she added as Lissa held her breath, a little flame of hope igniting at Darla's phrasing, "even if he agreed to take me on as a substitute for you, I have some real problems with doing it . . . not to mention that it's very doubtful I could get along with your brother long enough to make the whole thing worthwhile."

The flame of hope began to dim.

"However," Darla said, her expression grim as she reached for her coat and started putting it on, "I'll think about it. There's a reason why I might be persuaded to go against my common sense and give it a try."

Lissa's face lighted up like sunshine, but as she came to her feet, Darla held up a hand in a cautioning gesture.

"But don't get your hopes up," she said warningly. "If things work out the way I hope they will, I'm not going to be interested in your proposition . . . in spite of the fact that I'd like to help *you* out."

The implication was clear that Darla didn't give a fig about helping Danny out, but Lissa didn't care. It wasn't as much as she'd hoped for, but there was still a chance Darla would agree, and that was better than nothing.

"Have you got a number where I can reach you?" Darla asked. She had her purse in her hand now, and it was obvious she was about to leave.

"Yes," Lissa said eagerly, snatching up her own purse to find a pen and a piece of paper. When she handed the slip to Darla, Darla frowned at it.

"You aren't based here in New York?" she asked.

"Boston," Lissa acknowledged. "That's where we grew up, and it's Harvard Medical School I want to attend."

Darla looked at her with humorous respect. "Well, I admit, I don't understand someone in your position wanting to throw what you've got away in order to be a doctor, but to each his own, I always say."

"So do I," Lissa responded gloomily as Darla started walking to the door, pausing there with one hand on the knob.

"I'll call you when I have a definite answer for you," she said, her expression softening as she looked at Lissa's woebegone expression, "but it might be wise for you to go on auditioning other singers."

Lissa shook her head. "I'm going back to Boston tomorrow," she sighed. "And anyway, I'm temporarily discouraged. I think I'll just wait until I see what you decide to do."

"Well, perhaps I'll accept your offer," Darla said thoughtfully, "though I'd be less than honest if I didn't tell you that there are reasons why I hope I won't have to."

Lissa was puzzled, but Darla straightened and lifted a hand in farewell.

"I've enjoyed talking to you," she said in a sincere manner, then stepped through the door and disappeared into the outer room.

For a while, Lissa remained in the studio, gazing out one of its grimy windows at nothing. She felt so frustrated she could scream. But after glancing at her watch, she saw that she didn't have time to scream. She had to grab a bite to eat, then rush to the nightclub for their performance.

As Lissa caught a taxi to take her back to her hotel where she would have room service while getting into the costume and makeup she would wear that night, she had her fingers crossed, though she knew she was foolish to hope that Darla would rescue her. But she was determined that if Darla should agree to replace her, Danny Farrell wasn't going to get away with sabotaging the substitution. He might not like it, but he was darned well going to put up with it. It was either that or have no singer at all, for Lissa had made up her mind she had put her own life on hold for Danny's sake as long as was fair. It was her turn now . . . or at least it would be if Darla Simmons made it possible.

She was smiling as she stepped out of the cab and paid the driver because she had figured out that if everything went well, she could resume her education at the beginning of the semester in January. She refused to contemplate where she would be if everything didn't go well. That was too much disappointment to bear for the moment.

CHAPTER FOUR

Sonny felt rather like a kid playing hooky as he ducked out of the New York hotel where the internists' mini-medical convention was being held and walked rapidly away down the street. But he had only recently attended an intensive course at his own hospital concerning the newest developments in treating cardiovascular disease, and he very much doubted the physician about to lecture on the subject back at the hotel, could tell him anything he didn't already know.

As Sonny got further away from the hotel, he slowed his pace until he was merely strolling along, enjoying the crisp fall weather, and the unaccustomed sense of freedom from responsibilities. As he approached Macy's, he remembered that Maggie had asked him to bring her back a present, and though he very much doubted she would appreciate anything he chose for her—their tastes at this stage in Maggie's development were so far apart as to be laughable—he nevertheless entered the store.

Buying Maggie clothes was out of the question. Sonny knew she would merely curl her lip at his conservative choices and stick whatever he purchased at the back of her closet as a meal for the resident moths. In fact, he thought her request for a present had probably been made more out of habit than conscious thought, since from the time she had learned to talk, she'd always asked him to bring her something back when he traveled.

Today, however, Sonny was in luck. After no more than five minutes in the store, he spotted a display of remarkably lifelike stuffed black-and-white panda bears which brought a smile even from the adults who spotted them. Ten minutes later, Sonny, in an excellent mood, was back on the street with one of the bears under his arm, where he immediately ran into one of his colleagues, who was also playing hooky from the lecture.

"Oops!" Frank Mathers grinned at him mischievously. "Caught in the act! So even a staid scion of Boston can't stomach one of Johnny Fillmore's meandering, deadly boring tours into the cardiovascular system, hmm?"

Sonny liked Frank, a devil-may-care bachelor who took nothing seriously in life other than the practice of medicine. He didn't necessarily approve of Frank's life-style—Frank was good-naturedly accused by the nurses at the hospital where he practiced of having the fastest hands in the East, and they weren't speaking of his medical prowess—but Sonny liked Frank for his ability to not only have a good time himself, but to lighten the atmosphere for everyone else around him as well.

"You've got it," Sonny replied with an amiable smile. "Whoever picked old John as one of the lecturers at this meeting must have been desperate."

"They were." Frank nodded, a twinkling look in his merry blue eyes. "I turned them down. And if you say 'shame on you,'" he added quickly when he saw the look on Sonny's face, "I'll deck you right here on the street. I don't get to come to New York anytime I please the way you do, and I have no intention of wasting my opportunities."

Sonny shrugged, though Frank was exaggerating about his ability to come to New York whenever he pleased, and Frank's face suddenly lit up with an idea.

"Speaking of opportunities," he said with a big grin, "how would you like to get out of going to that godawful banquet they're having tonight and have some real fun?"

At first, Sonny was a little leery of whatever Frank might have in mind, but on second thought, he decided he was definitely not in the mood for a dull dinner, and though Frank might get out of line sometimes, occasionally he came up with something worth doing.

"What'd you have in mind?" he attempted to find out which category Frank's suggestion was going to fall in this time.

The twinkle in Frank's eyes grew more wicked. "I ain't talkin'," he said, clearly laughing internally at Sonny's cautious attitude. "But if you're interested in some fun instead of being bored out of your mind tonight, meet me in the lobby about seven. I know a great Italian restaurant where we can fuel up for the evening, and then I'll treat you to some entertainment that'll blow your mind."

"That's what I'm afraid of," Sonny drawled in a dry tone. But then, feeling unaccountably reckless, he shrugged and smiled. "But you're on," he agreed. "I can't stomach another piece of rubber chicken."

Frank laughed and slapped Sonny on the shoulder. "Good for you!" he boomed heartily. "Meanwhile, I'm going shopping for some lingerie for a sweet little nurse who has so far resisted my charm, but whom I expect to overwhelm any day now."

"If she's the type to resist your so-called charm, I doubt if she'll be interested in the type of lingerie you'll pick out," Sonny responded with dry humor.

Frank was undeterred. "Still waters run deep, my friend," he quipped as he started backing away. "Mark my words . . . the ladies who are the most reserved on the surface are usually tigers when you manage to strip away their defenses . . . and I do mean *strip away,*" he added with a good-humored leer.

Sonny merely shook his head, but as usual, his friend left him with a smile on his face, and his good mood lasted throughout the rest of the afternoon, which he spent at the Metropolitan Museum.

As Lissa stepped out of the tiny cramped dressing room at the club where the Freaky Foursome was to perform that night, she was feeling less resentful than usual at the prospect of having to spend her time cavorting on a stage when she would rather be studying anatomy. She had decided to be optimistic about Darla Simmons's response to the offer she'd made. There would be time enough to be depressed if Darla didn't come through. Meanwhile, she would do the best she could to keep from letting Danny down, in case he later had to suffer from what he would no doubt consider utter betrayal by his own flesh and blood.

Tonight, Lissa wore a lavender wig that matched her eyes, the usual dark eye makeup she adopted to help conceal her features, purple lipstick and blush to match the purple boa she had recovered from Jay, a revealing lavender camisole top and a calf-length dark purple tight skirt with a slit up to her thighs. She also wore lavender bobbysox and red-sequined high heels.

Passing a mirror in the narrow hallway leading to the stage, Lissa caught a full-length glimpse of herself, shuddered, and quickly averted her eyes. Jay appeared by her side at that moment and caught her reaction to her appearance.

Grinning, he threw an arm over her shoulders and gave her a hug. "You look smashing, love," he teased her, knowing she despised her appearance.

"I'd like to smash something all right," Lissa muttered, and then grimaced as she got a look at Jay's costume.

He was in a tight leopard-skin outfit tonight, and though Jay was naturally thin, he was also wirily fit. The costume he wore showed off his muscles.

"Ah . . . ah . . . ah!" he held up an admonishing finger at seeing Lissa's grimace and waved it in front of her face. "You know the old saying: if you can't say something nice—"

"Then I won't say anything at all," Lissa responded, a slight smile appearing on her purple lips when Jay feigned hurt feelings.

Jerry Madison joined them then, the only one of the group who dressed relatively conservatively in jeans and a red T-shirt that had *drummer* framed by two drumsticks written across the front of it. Jerry explained that the logo was for the benefit of those in the audience who weren't familiar with band instruments and needed help identifying what he did.

Jerry was, in fact, the most basically conservative member of the Freaky Foursome, excluding Lissa, of course. A devoted husband and father, he said he played with the band because he was good at it, he needed the money for his family, and he had been friends with Danny and Jay since grade school and didn't want to let them down.

"Hi, guys," he said calmly, his dark eyes passing over Lissa's and Jay's weird costumes without expression. "You seen Danny yet?"

"He's working on the amplifiers," Jay explained. "This place is too small to blast 'em full force. Gotta tone it down."

"Thank goodness." Lissa nodded. She had always hated being in an audience where the entertainment threatened to deafen one permanently, and becoming a member of the Freaky Foursome hadn't changed her view.

Danny joined them a few minutes later, his handsome face taut with the tension he always displayed before a performance.

"Everybody set?" he asked, inspecting his group with blue eyes that contrasted sharply with his dark hair and coloring and added to his physical appeal enormously.

Lissa nodded along with Jay and Jerry as she performed an inspection of her own on her brother. Tonight, he wore a a yellow sweatband to hold back his black hair and a yellow T-shirt under one of the many white Italian-style jackets he owned. His long, muscular legs were encased in skintight blue jeans and he wore elaborately embossed cowboy boots.

"Keep the volume down," Danny instructed them tensely. "The audience won't be all that young, probably, and with the size of this place, we'll blast them out of their chairs if we play the way we normally do."

Since this gig was a personal favor for a friend of Danny's and the recompense would barely cover expenses, Jay and Jerry weren't all that concerned with whether their performance went over big with the audience or not. But Danny couldn't abide the thought of giving less than his best to any audience, and the rest of the group knew he would ream them out royally if they didn't perform up to standard.

The four of them came onstage to the sound of swelling applause, and as usual, Danny's wide grin charmed the women in the audience, as did his husky, sexy voice when he said a few words of introduction.

Lissa stood at a standup microphone adjacent to Danny with one hand on her jauntily cocked hip and the other hand holding her tambourine at her side, while she grinned at the audience, too, though whoever was working the lights was blinding her and she couldn't see anything other than a bunch of silhouettes sitting at tables grouped around the stage. Not that she really cared to see the faces of those gaping up at her. Unlike Danny, who seemed to receive some psychic charge from interacting with the audience, Lissa always felt uncomfortable with being on display for the first few moments of a performance, at least until she settled down to do her job. Therefore, she was completely unaware that there was one member of this particular audience who was in something of a state of shock at finding himself at yet another performance of the Freaky Foursome.

Sonny Strotherton sat at a table beside Frank Mathers trying very hard to look relaxed so that Frank wouldn't suspect how much conflict he was experiencing at seeing the Vixen again. In her wild costume, she looked as ridiculous as she had the first time he'd seen her, but now Sonny started unconsciously looking past the makeup and the clothes and inspecting Lissa's excellent figure.

While he was deciding that it was a shame to encase such a beautiful frame in such an unflattering costume, he was also hoping she wouldn't sing the one song that he still sneaked downstairs to play even while telling himself he was going completely round the bend to do so.

Concentrate on the exterior, Sonny, he told himself somewhat grimly as Lissa and Danny started singing one of their duets. *Forget the voice and forget the words of that damned song. Otherwise, you'd better start thinking about looking up a shrink and getting straightened out!*

As was true in most families, Lissa's and Danny's voices were capable of blending into an incredible match of complementary tones, and as Sonny sat in the audience and listened more intently than he would have preferred to, he was struck again by how talented these garish-looking performers were. But though Sonny heard two voices, he had eyes for only one of the singers. It bewildered him that he could actually be attracted to such a bizarre-looking woman, and he set about studying the Vixen with the intense concentration of a scientist faced with a problem that had no logical solution on the surface, but must have one somewhere if he could only discover it.

But there was nothing to see, if one discounted the svelte lines of Lissa's figure which the costume she wore couldn't disguise, except a revolting exterior that in Sonny's opinion shouldn't have appealed to any man other than a complete maniac. So why did his brain insist upon remembering how lovely her eyes were up close and the impression of innate dignity he'd gotten at seeing the Vixen backstage when he'd had Maggie with him?

Frank noticed Sonny shaking his head in bewildered self-disgust and misinterpreted the gesture to mean that Sonny didn't appreciate the entertainment in the least. Grinning, he leaned closer and lifted an elbow to jab Sonny in the ribs. Sonny winced and glared at Frank, who only grinned wider.

"Forget you're a blueblooded member of the Boston nobility for a change and loosen up," Frank whispered. "Don't be such a stuffed shirt, Sonny boy. These guys are good."

Sonny hated to be called *Sonny boy,* but he didn't reveal his inner feelings to Frank. Instead, he merely shrugged and returned his attention to the stage, trying to pretend his eyes weren't being pulled there as though they were attached to a magnet.

The performance was three-quarters over, and Sonny was beginning to feel relieved, since it looked as though the Vixen wasn't going to sing the song he'd dreaded to hear, when two things happened simultaneously. The inept lighting technician made another mistake and turned the lights full on the audience, revealing Sonny to Lissa's heretofore uninterested gaze, and Danny announced that Lissa would now sing, "You're the Only Man for Me."

Both Sonny and Lissa immediately tensed up, Sonny because he was trying to gird himself to resist the particular appeal of that particular song, Lissa for no reason she could adequately explain to herself at first. But as the group played through the introduction, she quickly decided she was only reacting to surprise at seeing someone she'd met before. And it didn't help that this particular someone was handsome enough to make almost any woman give him a second glance.

As Lissa automatically starting half-singing, half-speaking the first words of her song, she remembered how the man in the audience had reacted the last time she'd sung it, and an imp of devilment seized her. She waited, looking everywhere but at Sonny, until the chorus came up. And then, as she had done once before accidentally, this time she deliberately returned her gaze to Sonny and sang the words, "You're the only man for me . . . the *only* man for me," directly to him, putting everything she had into her voice and look, before she looked away from him again.

When Sonny had surfaced from the gut-wrenching impact of what Lissa had done, he became aware that Frank was gazing at him with an odd look on his face.

If Sonny had ever blushed in his life, he couldn't remember it. It was therefore infuriating to feel his face heating up with embarrassment under the onslaught of Frank's curious gaze. Fortunately, the man in charge of lighting for the performance had by now corrected his error and the audience was once again bathed in dim anonymity while the stage was blazing with light.

Leaning close, Frank inclined his head toward the stage and whispered, "Do you know her?"

"Of course not!" Sonny snapped under his breath, and immediately wished he hadn't protested so strongly. Frank's sly grin seemed to indicate he was unconvinced. Sonny was therefore grateful when Frank came back with a whispered comment that denied this conclusion.

"I guess she's just taken with those aristocratic good looks of yours then," he joked, and Sonny merely shrugged one shoulder in a bored fashion by way of reply.

Inwardly, he was anything but bored, however. He was physically aroused, mentally incredulous that his body was reacting to the little vamp up on the stage in such a stupid, uncontrollable manner, and emotionally, he was completely at sea. In all his predictable life, he had never felt out of control. Now he did, and he hated the feeling. Hated it and feared it and yet couldn't seem to win back the self-possession he had maintained for as long as he could remember.

By the end of the Freaky Foursome's performance, Sonny was absolutely furious . . . and just as absolutely determined to put a stop to whatever was going on that was causing him such unbearable discomfort.

Frank, apparently, was prepared to stay at the table drinking and talking until the club closed. Sonny had no intention of doing anything of the kind. He considered using a trip to the men's room as an excuse to do what he had in mind, then rejected the idea since Frank might come with him.

"Frank, I've got to go call Maggie and make sure she's all right," he said as he got to his feet. "Order me another Manhattan, will you?"

Before Frank could reply, Sonny walked away as rapidly as possible without breaking into an all-out run, and when he was in the club's lobby, he headed backstage, only to be stopped by a burly man in a tuxedo.

"Nobody's allowed back here," the man grunted at him, and from the look in the man's flat gray eyes, Sonny quickly decided it would be useless to try to brush past him.

"I'm a friend of the Foursome," he said with casual aplomb as he fished in his pocket for some money.

The man who barred his way watched Sonny take the cash out of his pocket, and there was a slight flicker of interest in his eyes, but his reply was still uncompromising.

"That's what they all say," he growled.

Sonny paused, then shrugged. "Will you at least take a note to . . . ah . . . the Vixen, then?" he asked, extending the roll of bills toward the man. "I'm sure she'll see me."

The man reached for the money and stuffed it in his pocket without saying anything while Sonny again fished in his pocket and found a pad of prescription forms with his name imprinted on them and a pen.

Quickly, he wrote, "My daughter Maggie and I met you backstage at the charity concert you gave in Boston recently. May I see you for a few moments?"

He gave the note to the bouncer who took it reluctantly, and gave Sonny a hard stare.

"Wait here," he grated and disappeared through the door behind him.

Lissa was seated before the mirror in her dressing room in a white silk wraparound robe taking off her lavender wig when she heard a knock on her door. Thinking it was one of the group, she called out, "Come in," and started running her fingers through her natural hair. The wigs always made her scalp itch. She froze when she saw the hulking form of the club bouncer appear in the mirror as the door opened and quickly forced herself not to turn around.

"Yes?" she said, putting a note of annoyed impatience into her tone.

"Got a note for you," the bouncer announced in his normal gruff tone as he came into the room. "Some fancy-dressed admirer of yours, I guess."

Lissa reached up over her shoulder to take the note and blanched when she saw that it was written on a prescription form. After scanning the words on it rapidly with her eyes, she felt panicky and cursed her idiotic sense of humor which was about to result in disaster for her if this Dr. Strotherton ever found out who she was.

"No, I don't . . ." she automatically started to say that she didn't want to see the man who had written this note, but then she heard footsteps outside the dressing room and some instinct told her that Dr. Strotherton hadn't waited for her permission to come backstage and see her.

Ducking her head, Lissa grabbed the lavender wig she'd tossed onto the makeup table, quickly dragged it on and started tucking stray wisps of her black hair underneath it while she watched her mirror with anxious eyes. Just as she'd feared, Dr. Fenwick Strotherton's image appeared there almost immediately.

The bouncer saw it, too, and with a ferocious scowl on his ugly face, he clenched his huge hands into fists and swung around to face Sonny.

"I told you to wait!" he said in a menacing tone as he started lumbering in Sonny's direction.

It was clear to Lissa that the goon had every intention of braining her unwanted visitor if she didn't stop him and she quickly did so.

"It's all right!" she said hastily as she continued to tuck her natural hair under the lavender wig. "I'll see him!"

The bouncer stopped and gave her a look of disgust over his shoulder. "Make up your mind!" he muttered, and with another scowl at Sonny, who had every muscle in his body tensed in order to parry the blow it looked like the bouncer had been about to deliver, the bouncer lumbered out of the room and shut the door behind him.

While Sonny relaxed his muscles and returned his gaze to Lissa,

Lissa glanced quickly in the mirror to satisfy herself that she had hidden every strand of her natural hair under the wig. Uttering a fast, silent prayer of gratitude that she hadn't been caught flat out, she stood up and turned around to face Sonny with a nervous smile on her lips.

"Well . . . hello . . . ," she said, almost wincing when she heard how awkward she sounded. Her natural poise was in complete disarray.

"Hello." Sonny nodded, his blue gaze wary as he inspected her, thinking the robe she wore was a hundred-percent improvement over her stage attire but her face and hair were still a mess. "Sorry I burst in on you like this, but I was afraid that hulk would take the tip I gave him and pocket it without giving you my message."

"Oh . . . no . . . ," Lissa quavered and clenched her hands to try to get a stronger grip on her panic. "He gave it to me," she managed to finish in a more normal tone, though her smile was still a little stiff.

Sonny relaxed slightly, let his mouth curve into a smile and took a step forward. Lissa just stopped herself from taking a step back when she realized she would end up trapped against the makeup table.

"How's your daughter?" she asked quickly as she casually moved to one side, away from the makeup table. "Is she keeping up her grades?"

Sonny was pleasantly surprised that the Vixen even remembered Maggie, or himself for that matter. Then he clamped down on the pleasure as he remembered what he'd come here for.

"She's doing fine," he answered in a level tone.

As Sonny spoke, he let his eyes roam Lissa's body in a way that made a wary shiver of pleasure trace her back. She quickly decided that if she wasn't careful, she could end up in trouble with this man. He was entirely too appealing for his, or her, own good, and for an instant, Lissa felt downright resentful that she had to find a way to get rid of him as quickly as possible. But she wasn't really the Vixen—she was a woman who wanted to become a doctor in the city of Boston . . . where this man already practiced.

"I'm glad." She nodded, taking another sideways step to put even more distance between herself and Sonny. "And it's nice to see you again, Dr. . . . uh . . ." She glanced at the note he'd sent her as though she didn't remember his name and immediately felt amused when she noticed for the first time that his Christian name was Fenwick.

"Strotherton," Sonny said in a wry way that Lissa liked. *"Sonny* Strotherton."

Forgetting her purpose for a moment, Lissa looked at him in a solemnly teasing way. "Not Fenwick?" she inquired gravely.

Sonny grimaced. "That's a family name," he admitted, "which, if I ever have a son, will hopefully end with my generation. I would never curse one of my children with such a handicap."

His mention of having a son provoked Lissa into inquiring, "And how does your wife feel about having another child when Maggie must be . . . what . . . about twelve?"

Sonny smiled at her in a way that made Lissa's heartrate speed up.

"I'm a widower," he said simply. "I meant I'd like to have more children if I ever marry again."

"Oh." Lissa just managed to keep her sudden upswelling of relief from reverberating in her voice as she became caught up in the invitation in Sonny's beautiful blue eyes and almost got lost there. Some stray wisp of self-preservation asserted itself fortunately before she forgot entirely that she needed to get rid of Sonny Strotherton . . . fast!

"I was wondering if you'd care to come out with me for a bite to eat," Sonny found himself saying when he hadn't been wondering any such thing at all. He was immediately annoyed at having voiced the invitation spontaneously, another indication of the lack of control this woman provoked in him.

But then Sonny realized that if the Vixen did agree to come out with him, she would surely have to take off all that makeup as well as the hideous lavender wig she was wearing, in which case he would be able to see what she really looked like. And maybe she wore all that makeup because her natural appearance left a lot to be desired, he thought hopefully, in which case he might be able to get her off his mind once and for all.

Lissa was stumped for a reply for a second and thoroughly annoyed at how much she would have liked to take Sonny Strotherton up on his invitation. Then an idea popped into her head she thought might just work to convince Sonny to retract this particular invitation as well as any future ones he might have been thinking of extending. She didn't consider it exactly fair that in order to preserve her identity she had to deprive herself of the chance to get to know this strikingly handsome man better, but she had given up expecting life to be fair when she'd lost her father. Besides, she reminded herself glumly, even if she could have accepted the invitation, there was no time in her life right now, and wouldn't be for a long time to come, to get involved with any man.

"Why, sweetie, what a *lovely* idea!" she gushed and batted her eyes at Sonny, certain he wasn't the sort of man to react favorably to such an approach. "And if this were another night, I'd say 'yes' like that!" She snapped her fingers and winked at him. "In fact," she added with as close as she knew how to come to a female leer, "if I hadn't already promised the owner of this club a little personal attention to pay him back for giving us a gig here tonight, I'd not only come out with you for dinner, I'd take you back to my hotel with me for the same sort of personal attention I have to give another man as a payoff . . . only with you, it would be a case of pure pleasure."

Lissa put her hands on her hips, spread her legs, thrust her breasts provocatively at Sonny and caught her bottom lip between her teeth while she gazed into his eyes with a smoldering expression she hardly had to fake, much to her disgust.

Sonny wondered if the Vixen often had to pay with personal favors to gain opportunities for her group to perform, a situation that filled him with pity for her . . . until he realized she didn't seem to mind the situation all that much. It made him sick. The lovely violet eyes he remembered from the last time he'd met this woman, the gentleness she had displayed then, were forgotten as he looked at the lust in her eyes and the brazen display she was making of her body.

Lissa saw the disgust and contempt come into Sonny's clear blue eyes and had to fight to maintain the role she had deliberately chosen with the objective of obtaining exactly such a reaction from him. But it wasn't easy to have him view her so negatively. In fact, it hurt so much, she had to use the burst of anger that abruptly filled her at finding herself in such a position as energy to complete the task she'd set herself.

"Maybe another time, sweetie, hmm?" she cooed at Sonny as she raised a hand to fiddle with a strand of the lavender wig and started walking toward him in an exaggeratedly sexy way. "My group is going out of town tomorrow, but why don't you keep track of us, and sometime when we're in this area again, you just send me another of those cute little notes, and I'll be sure and make time for you."

Sonny held his ground when Lissa stopped only a breath away from him, though his first reaction was to move away from her before she could reach out and touch him.

Lissa saw what he was thinking in his eyes, and suddenly her anger burgeoned into something closer to rage. Even if she was everything she'd made him believe she was, what right did he have to hold her in such contempt? she wondered bitterly. Was he so lily white and pure that he felt her touch would contaminate him?

Acting with complete spontaneity, Lissa moved before Sonny could stop her, grasping his handsome face between her hands and coming up on tiptoe to fasten her mouth to his with a strength Sonny was powerless to counteract for a moment.

A bare few seconds after her mouth met Sonny's, however, Lissa realized her mistake and tried to break away just as suddenly as she'd initiated the kiss. Her anger gone, her eyes wide, she was abruptly aware that this was not a man she could play such a game with and win. His mouth on hers had instigated a sensation as violent as an electric shock and as tempting as obtaining paradise on earth.

Sonny's initial reaction to Lissa's touch was repulsion, but as he put his hands on her hips to push her away, he felt the heat of her body beneath the silk, which made him pause for an instant. His eyes were open and when Lissa's eyes opened wide in shock at what she was feeling, he saw again the lovely shade of violet, the intelligence behind the beauty, and a vulnerability that erased from his mind the role she had just played for him as though it had never happened.

As Lissa began to pull away, Sonny acted as spontaneously as she had in kissing him in the first place and quickly stopped her. Sliding his arms around her waist, he quickly pulled her hard against his body and simultaneously opened his mouth over hers in an invasive kiss that sent another thrilling shock through Lissa. Desperately, she fought to counteract the eruption of passion inside her, but it was as though Sonny didn't even feel her hands pushing against his shoulders, and before another moment had gone by, Lissa couldn't concentrate on what she *should* be doing anymore. She was too intently involved in heeding the call of senses she had never suspected any man could ignite with such devastating passion.

Sonny's long spell of celibacy accelerated the blind hunger that consumed him now. Later, he would also suspect that the Vixen had tapped a dark, deeply hidden side of him every man might have to some degree or another—the desire to have a sexual liaison with a woman so wanton she had none of the inhibitions the average woman might. For while what he had seen in Lissa's eyes as she recognized the impact their kiss was having on her had chased away his initial revulsion toward her, he was also on some level still reacting to the brazen act she had put on before she had kissed him.

Lissa gasped against his mouth as Sonny's hands moved with urgent forcefulness to her buttocks and he held her tight against him as he began to grind his hips against hers, heightening the swelling heat in his loins and provoking a conflicting reaction in Lissa's mind and body. For while the action sent the heat of her passion surging through her veins like a powerful drug, her mind protested the lack of any emotional sensitivity in Sonny which would legitimize his graphic lovemaking.

But Sonny's kiss erased the protest Lissa's mind was trying to make. Lissa could only submit as his lips devoured hers and his tongue probed the secrets of her mouth with urgent possessiveness.

There was no question where the lovemaking would have ended if Jay hadn't rapped on her door and called out, "Get a move on, babe! You know Danny doesn't like to wait."

Sonny went still and opened his eyes. As he looked at the heavy black makeup around Lissa's closed lids, the lavender wig, and the purple lipstick that was now smudged around her mouth, he felt as though he were coming out of a dream . . . a nightmare perhaps. His body was still throbbing with a need he couldn't quickly control, but the rest of him was appalled that he had been making violent love to a woman who was about to pay off this Danny with her body. How many other men had she responded to as wholeheartedly as she'd just responded to his own lovemaking?

Sonny let Lissa go so abruptly, she stumbled backward before catching her balance. And as she straightened, now staring up at him with a dazed look in her large violet eyes, he quickly turned away so as not to be caught again in the trap of that deceptive innocence and vulnerability she could adopt so readily.

He left the dressing room without another word, failing to remember that Frank Mathers was still waiting for him until he was two blocks away from the club. Then, uttering a sharp curse, he reluctantly retraced his steps, only to find that Frank had somehow managed to snag himself a date with a cocktail waitress while Sonny had been gone. Relieved, Sonny said a quick good night and this time caught a cab at the club's entrance to take him back to his hotel where he would spend the rest of the night trying to make sense out of what had happened between him and a woman he now wanted no part of.

Meanwhile, Lissa, after numbly going through the motions of removing her makeup and wig and dressing in street clothes, then joining the rest of the Foursome for the ride back to their hotel, lay in her hotel room bed vainly trying to blank her mind against remembering what Dr. Sonny Strotherton's lovemaking had aroused in her.

Toward dawn, she finally found some peace by concentrating on the fact that regardless of what had happened, it was now over. And if the look on Sonny Strotherton's face when he'd pushed her away from him was any indication, he would never seek her out after one of the Freaky Foursome's appearances again.

The only worry that still prevented her from obtaining the rest her body needed was that there was a small chance she would meet Sonny again when she was at last a member of the Boston medical community. But that was so far in the future, if it should occur at all, that Sonny would no doubt be married by then. Lissa had managed to dismiss her worries by the time she had to get up and meet the group for the trip back to Boston.

Only Jay commented on her red-rimmed eyes and general air of exhaustion when they met in the hotel lobby that morning.

"Been up hitting the medical books all night?" he inquired lightly as he raised her chin to peer at her face with amused interest.

Lissa pulled her chin out of his grip and shook her head without meeting his eyes. "I just hate staying in hotels," she said sourly, which wasn't really a lie. She did sleep badly on the road.

Jay grimaced and left her alone then, and Lissa determinedly turned her thoughts toward the comforts of home, with an occasional fervent detour toward the hope that Darla Simmons would rescue her soon from a life she was finding even more difficult to tolerate than usual.

CHAPTER FIVE

In the middle of the dream he was having, just at the point where he was about to make passionate love to the Vixen, Sonny abruptly came awake, feeling both astonished and confused by the betrayal of his subconscious.

"What the hell?" he muttered groggily. And though it certainly was not the first time in his life he'd had a sexual dream, this time he felt almost embarrassed over it.

Sonny got up, went to the bathroom, drank a glass of water, stared disgruntledly at his stubbled face in the mirror and tried to think logically about what his subconscious was trying to tell him.

"Just because she's not the type of woman I would want as a mate when awake and in full possession of my faculties, it doesn't mean she isn't harmless fantasy material," he muttered to himself as he set the empty glass down on the cabinet and retraced his steps back to bed.

You've had enough psychology courses to know that fantasies have no bearing on what a person wants in reality, man, he addressed himself with stubborn perseverance as he lay staring up at the dark ceiling. *And maybe you're hitting male menopause a few years early,* he added with self-mocking humor. *Or, since you never kicked over the traces when you were younger, maybe you're going through a stage of delayed adolescence instead of male menopause.*

He was wide awake now and unable to get back to sleep, much to his disgust. He'd learned long ago the value to a physician of snatching uninterrupted rest when the opportunity presented itself. But since sleep was impossible for the time being, Sonny continued to mull over his present attachment, even if the attachment was only subconscious, to a woman who was totally outside his experience.

Sonny knew his daughter, and perhaps other people as well, considered him a complete square . . . and with good reason. He couldn't remember a time growing up when he'd felt the need to rebel seriously against the authority of his parents. Instead, knowing at a young age that he wanted to be a physician, he had concentrated intensely on his studies, though he did go out for football, baseball, and basketball and had been reasonably competent at all three sports.

He had also dated as much as his peers, and though he hadn't come out of high school a virgin, neither had he dedicated himself to scoring with every girl he took out, as most of his male friends seemed to have done, and some still did. Frank Mathers, for example, though in his mid-thirties, still seemed stuck in that frenzied adolescent quest for ever new and better sexual partners.

College hadn't been that much different. He had met Caroline, a doctor's daughter who understood his goals, during his junior year at Harvard, and they had gone steady until graduation, then married before Sonny entered medical school. Since Sonny had genuinely loved and respected Caroline and their relationship had been reasonably fulfilling, it had never entered his head to cheat on her, in spite of the opportunities that steadily came his way. But even if he and his wife hadn't been so compatible, he doubted he would have sought excitement elsewhere. It just wasn't his style. It wasn't honorable.

His style and his honor hadn't changed much since losing his wife and growing older either, though his long-term celibacy was beginning to take its toll. He was going to take his vacation in the Caribbean soon, without Maggie, and with every intention of doing something about easing his problem.

So maybe simple physical need had contributed to his making mad, passionate love to a violet-eyed harpy in his sleep, but it didn't exactly explain why his subconscious had chosen such an unsuitable companion . . . unless that kiss he and the Vixen had exchanged had gotten to him more than he'd realized.

Frowning, Sonny mentally relived his previous encounters with the

Vixen, ending with a recapitulation of the kiss in her dressing room and the memory of it had stirred him again.

"Okay," he muttered irritably to himself. "So there's something about her that calls to the animal in you. So what? You can't help your dreams, damn it, so stop stewing over them and let your subconscious do whatever the hell it likes!"

With that conclusion, Sonny pounded his pillow with a fist, settled himself comfortably, and finally managed to sleep again. He was somewhat sheepishly relieved, however, when upon waking the next morning, he couldn't remember any more dreams.

The ringing of the telephone brought Elizabeth groggily awake, and she fumbled the receiver off the hook and muttered a sleepy, "Hello."

"Miss Farrell? Lissa?" a vaguely familiar feminine voice came over the line.

"Mmm." Elizabeth made a confirming noise.

"This is Darla Simmons," the voice replied.

Elizabeth was blank for a moment, then abruptly opened her eyes as her mind settled on who Darla Simmons was and what she might mean to Elizabeth's future.

"Darla!" she exclaimed as she pushed herself upright into a sitting position. "How are you?"

"Not so good," Darla replied in a dryly weary tone. "Is your offer about the singing job still open?"

Elizabeth's heart abruptly leapt with excited joy, but something in Darla's voice made her answer carefully.

"Of course, it's open," she said with only a trace of the eagerness she was feeling, "but is there something wrong, Darla? You sound terrible."

"Oh, it's just that . . . But never mind," Darla said heavily. "It's nothing you need to concern yourself with."

"Maybe not," Elizabeth answered gently, "but I'm willing to listen if you need to talk."

Darla hesitated, then said, with a shrug in her voice, "Well, I guess it's only fair that you know why I'm accepting your offer. I'm doing it for the money, Lissa. My mother's ill. She needs an operation, and she doesn't have any medical insurance. Besides, there's some controversy over whether the operation is necessary. So she needs my help."

"Oh, Darla, I'm sorry," Elizabeth said sincerely. Then, unable to suppress her medical curiosity, she asked, "What's wrong with her, Darla? And who's treating her?"

"She has fibroid tumors in her uterus," Darla explained. "They're benign, but they're causing her a great deal of pain and bleeding."

"Then there shouldn't be any doubt that she needs the operation," Elizabeth commented.

"You wouldn't think so, but my mother is caught between one doctor who says she should have it and another who says she doesn't need it that there's no way she can get approved for financial help, and aside from the physical pain, she's emotionally upset. She doesn't know who to believe."

Elizabeth grimaced. "It sounds like she needs a third opinion," she suggested.

"Fat chance," Darla sighed. "She can't afford it."

"Where is your mother, Darla?" Elizabeth asked thoughtfully.

"Wichita, Kansas," Darla answered.

"Well, I've got contacts in the medical community, remember?" Elizabeth said in a soothing tone. "Let me see if I can find the name of a good gynecologist in Wichita who will be willing to wait for the money."

"Would you really do that?" Darla asked hopefully. "I mean, I'd really appreciate it, but I don't want you to have to go to a lot of trouble for someone you don't even know."

"Don't worry about it," Elizabeth said with cheerful firmness. She would have done the same for anyone, but it especially delighted her to be able to help Darla, who was the answer to a prayer. "Now," she added, changing the subject, "where are you, and how soon can you come to Boston?"

"I'm in New York City," Darla said, sounding relieved. "And I can be in Boston this afternoon."

"Wonderful!" Elizabeth said fervently. "I can meet you at Logan Airport."

"Oh, really, you don't have to . . . ," Darla started to say, but Elizabeth cut her off with a happy chuckle.

"Darla, believe me. It's no trouble at all. And don't worry about where you're going to stay, either. There's room here at my house. Now what time is your plane due in?"

A few minutes later, Elizabeth hung up the phone, and with a song on her lips and a sparkle of anticipation in her large eyes, she hopped out of bed to take a shower, dress, and figure out a plan of action to confront Danny with her successor.

"This isn't going to work," Darla said a few hours later as she stood in front of the mirror in Elizabeth's bedroom eyeing her Vixen costume and makeup. "I don't look enough like you, even with all the camouflage."

Elizabeth looked at her in astonishment. "You're kidding!" she exclaimed, switching her gaze to the image in the mirror. "You're a dead ringer for the Vixen."

Darla frowned. "Are you sure you're not just indulging in wishful thinking?" she said skeptically, peering closer at her own image.

"Well, it's possible, I suppose—" Elizabeth shrugged "—but I don't think so. And anyway, it doesn't matter what I think. The real test will be whether you can pull things off tonight."

Darla turned and grinned at Elizabeth, "Well, she said brightly, "in for a penny . . . in for a pound. Is it time to go yet?"

Elizabeth glanced at her watch just about the time a knock came on her bedroom door.

"Come on, sis!" Danny called impatiently, and Elizabeth was extremely grateful that she'd locked her door, for Danny was rattling the knob. "Get with it! We'll be late."

"I'll be with you in a minute!" Elizabeth called out. "Go start the car."

Elizabeth ran to her closet to get one of her coats for Darla to wear.

"Now, remember," she said as she held it while Darla slipped her arms in the sleeves. "Even if this blows up in our faces, it's no big deal. This is just an impromptu gig at the club that gave Danny his start. And I know he won't make a public scene even if he discovers that you're not me. He'll wait until he gets you home and take on both of us at once."

Darla rolled her eyes. "Thank goodness, he doesn't even know I exist yet. If he'd been home when you brought me here, he'd be wondering why I wasn't invited to come along for the show tonight."

"Why do you think I slipped you in here like a thief in the night?" Elizabeth said smugly. "This is the perfect opportunity to show Danny you can take my place. What can he say if you fool even him? He won't have a leg to stand on about protesting the arrangement."

"You seem to forget that I may not fool him," Darla said dryly. "If nothing else, I haven't had time to memorize all the songs the group does."

"If he wants to do something you don't know, improvise," Elizabeth suggested. "Or better yet, pretend you're coming down with appendicitis or something and make yourself scarce."

"You're a big help." Darla grimaced, but Elizabeth paid her no mind. Instead she pushed her toward the door of the bedroom.

Cautiously, Elizabeth opened the door and peered out to make sure the coast was clear. It was, and she shoved Darla out into the hall.

"Break a leg!" she whispered, then slammed the door between herself and the woman she fervently hoped was going to be a better Vixen than Elizabeth herself had ever hoped (or wanted) to be.

A few moments later, she watched from her window in her darkened bedroom as Danny's car sped down the street, and she breathed a heartfelt sigh of relief. So far, so good.

Then she settled down with one of her father's medical tomes and tried to concentrate on it while she waited to see if she was at last going to be released from Danny's dream and given the opportunity to pursue her own.

A few hours later, Elizabeth jerked awake in her chair when she heard voices outside in the hall . . . raised, angry voices that sent a chill down her spine. Then the door to her bedroom was shoved open and Danny, his face darkly thunderous, shoved Darla into the room in front of him. Jay and Jerry crowded in behind them.

"What the hell do you mean setting us up like that?!" Danny

demanded angrily. He ignored the furious look he was getting from Darla.

"Setting you up?" Elizabeth echoed faintly, trying to get her jumbled thoughts together and calm her racing heart so that she could hold her own in the fight. She got to her feet, then had to take a step backward as Danny paced forward.

"Don't play innocent with me!" he snarled. "You know what you did, and it was a disaster!"

Elizabeth frowned and glanced at Darla, Jay, and Jerry, in turn. She was encouraged that Darla looked stubbornly outraged at Danny's description, while Jay and Jerry looked not only embarrassed, but as though they disagreed with Danny's assessment.

Before she could answer her brother, Darla stepped forward.

"It was *not* a disaster!" she said heatedly. "You didn't have a clue I wasn't Lissa until you wanted to sing that new song I don't know yet, and . . ."

"I'll decide what works and what doesn't with the Foursome," Danny interrupted in a hostile voice, never taking his eyes from Elizabeth's face. "I just thought you weren't up to par tonight, that's all. I didn't realize it wasn't you until I started the intro to 'Fall Time' and you . . . she . . . didn't join in!"

"Baloney!" Darla snorted. "There wasn't a person in the audience who suspected a thing, and where do you get off saying I wasn't 'up to par'?" She turned to Jay and Jerry with a glare on her painted face. "What about you two? You know I was up to par, don't you?!"

Danny immediately turned and gave Jay and Jerry a menacing look of warning, whereupon his two partners squirmed.

"Well, actually, she wasn't bad, Danny boy," Jay said with courageous breeziness. "She had me fooled."

"Then you've got a tin ear!" Danny snarled, but when he turned back to face Elizabeth, she had assessed the situation and gathered her own courage. She wasn't about to let Danny's reluctance to face change spoil her chance.

"Come off it, Danny," she said with level firmness, looking him steadily in the eye. "Admit you were completely fooled until Darla didn't know the words to your new song."

"Never!" he said coldly. "Unlike some people, I have an excellent ear, and I knew from the beginning that there was something wrong with your voice tonight."

Knowing Danny's talents, Elizabeth suspected he was telling the truth . . . but that didn't mean he wasn't twisting the truth for his own benefit.

"All right, so you knew there was something different about my voice," she said with a shrug. "But different doesn't mean worse, does it? I've heard Darla sing myself, and while there might be a shade of difference in our voices, as far as I'm concerned, Darla's voice is as good or better than mine."

Danny didn't give an inch. His blue eyes fairly blazed with anger and determination.

"I repeat," he said gratingly. "I make the decisions where the Foursome is concerned, and I say she's not good enough."

Elizabeth seldom lost her temper, but she did now, and her violet eyes blazed right back at Danny.

"Then that's just too damned bad!" she stormed at her brother. "Because I'm finished with the Foursome, Danny, as of tonight! And if Darla isn't good enough, then you're stuck, brother dear, because it's either her or no one! You can make up your mind to that!"

Danny's expression changed as he began to take her seriously, but before he could begin one of his attacks on her better nature, Elizabeth cut him off.

"Jay . . . Jerry!" she demanded, stepping around Danny. "Tell the truth! Can Darla fill my shoes or do you two want to cancel all of your engagements for the next few years while you try to find someone to replace her?"

Jay and Jerry looked startled and dismayed. They exchanged a glance, then looked at Danny, who was glaring at them, but before they could answer, Darla stepped in again, her hostile gaze fixed on Danny's face as though she'd like to hit him.

"Maybe the question is academic, Lissa!" she snapped. "Maybe I wouldn't take this job if your high and mighty brother got down on his knees and begged me to!"

"Don't hold your breath!" Danny immediately responded, his expression and voice as hostile as Darla's.

Elizabeth was dismayed, but she forced herself not to show it.

"Whatever you say, Darla," she said calmly, and fixed her eyes steadily on Danny again. "But whatever Darla does or doesn't do, Danny, I'm through. And don't give me any of your smooth talk about family loyalty," she quickly added when she recognized the shifting expression in her brother's eyes. "You haven't been the least bit interested in displaying any of that loyalty you claim for yourself toward me. You've known how I feel all along, and you made me promises you had no intention of keeping. I wouldn't be surprised if you haven't auditioned even one person to take my place, much less the hundreds you claim to have seen."

Danny had the grace to look slightly guilty, but instead of apologizing, he merely shrugged his broad shoulders and attempted an explanation.

"I was going to," he said quietly. "I just needed a little more time. In six months or so . . ."

"In six months, I'll be in medical school," Elizabeth said equally as quietly, but with no lack of firmness. "Now, make a choice, Danny. Are you going to apologize to Darla and ask her to work with you, or are you going to shut everything down until you find a replacement for me? I warn you . . . unlike you, I *have* been holding auditions, and I can tell you, it isn't going to be easy to fill my shoes."

"You're telling me," Danny snorted. Then he stood for a moment, his firm jaw tensed, as he inspected Elizabeth's expression for any sign of weakening.

Elizabeth was careful not to give any such sign, and when Danny at last looked toward Darla, Elizabeth looked at her as well.

Darla was standing with her arms folded, staring back at Danny with no sign of weakening on her face either. Elizabeth felt a surge of affection for her. She was delighted that Darla wasn't the type to let Danny run all over her, the way most females did. All Danny usually had to do was smile or wink and his female companions forgot his latest show of neglect or bad temper as though it had never happened.

"Sorry, Darla," he said grudgingly, and then treated her to one of his devastating smiles. He seemed disconcerted when Darla didn't respond to his charm the way most other women did.

Darla stared hard at him for a moment, then spoke in a flat, convincing voice.

"You're not sorry at all, Danny Farrell, but I don't care. If you're offering me Lissa's job, I'll take it for reasons of my own. But don't think I'm desperate enough for it to put up with any disrespect or tyrannical behavior from you. I'll take your direction where music and the band are concerned, as long as it's given in a professional manner. But don't you ever speak to me the way you did earlier tonight again, or I'll walk out on you in the middle of a concert."

With that, Darla threw Elizabeth's coat onto her bed, stalked to the bathroom, and slammed the door behind her.

"Whew!" Jay said, trying to break the tension he felt quivering in the room. "She's a little fireball, isn't she?"

Danny gave him a hard, disgusted look, then turned back to Elizabeth.

"It wasn't right to do this to me, Elizabeth."

"On the contrary, it was the only way," Elizabeth countered quietly. "If I'd tried to handle things in the normal manner, you wouldn't have given Darla or any other prospect a chance, and you know it. I think you should be grateful that I didn't leave you completely high and dry. This way, you can keep the Foursome's commitments, and you can keep them with honor. Darla won't let you down . . . as long as you don't let her down."

Typically, when faced with a situation he didn't like but couldn't change, Danny temporarily withdrew inside himself. Without answering Elizabeth, he shrugged his shoulders, and with a cold, distant look on his face, he left the room.

Jay and Jerry hesitated in the doorway.

"I'm sorry, fellows," Elizabeth said sincerely. "But I just had to get my life back. Surely you understand."

Jerry hesitated, then smiled at her and nodded.

"Sure, kid," he said affectionately. "In fact, when you get that medical degree, I'll bring my kids in to see you. If you're any good, you got some patients right off the bat."

Elizabeth grinned at him. "I'm going to be good, Jerry," she promised confidently. "There's no way I'm going to let Dad—or myself—or my patients down."

"I believe you, kid." Jerry shrugged, and lifting a hand in farewell, he left the room to go home to his family.

"Jay?" Elizabeth asked when she saw that Jay wasn't certain how he felt about the whole thing yet. "Don't you really think Darla can do it?"

"Oh, hell," Jay said flippantly. "Sure she can. It's just that, well, it doesn't matter all that much what I think. Danny's the one who needs convincing, and I don't look forward to his moods until he gets over what you did."

Elizabeth sighed and shook her head at him. "Jay, why is it that everyone spoils Danny?" she asked forlornly. "Oh, I do it, too," she admitted before he could respond. "But I'm not so sure it's good for him."

"Good for him or not, it's easier." Jay grinned wickedly. "But, like the rest of us mere mortals, I guess even he can't have everything his own way all the time. So don't worry, babe," he said, coming to give her a hug. "We'll get through this. And in spite of everything, I'm happy for you now that you're going to go after what you've always wanted."

"Thanks, Jay." Elizabeth smiled and reached up to kiss his cheek. But when Jay had gone, and before Darla came back into the room, she took a moment to brush a tear from her cheek as she wondered why Danny couldn't be happy for her as well . . . the way their mother and father would have been happy for her.

For the first time in a long while, Elizabeth wondered what it would be like to have one special person pulling for her, supporting her . . . sharing her triumphs and failures. But since that was out of the question for the time being, she put her wistful wonderings aside in favor of soothing Darla's feelings, feelings that Danny had trampled on as though they didn't exist.

CHAPTER SIX

As Elizabeth hurried toward her godfather's office in order to be on time for lunch with him, she felt better than she had since graduating from college—before her father had become ill and she'd had to put her goals on hold for far longer than she had suspected would be necessary at the time. She was back on track, free of any distractions or responsibilities other than concentrating totally on her studies.

Thank God for Uncle Ferris, she thought affectionately, as she entered the building where her godfather, Dr. Ferris Cabot, had his medical offices. *Without him to smooth the way for me, it might have been a lot harder to get accepted into Harvard a second time.*

Elizabeth wasn't really ignoring the fact that her grades in college were outstanding, nor that she'd had no difficulty collecting sponsorship from past associates of her father. But since Ferris Cabot was on the faculty as a part-time lecturer in pediatric medicine at Harvard, as well as having a solid reputation as a practicing physician in that field, his efforts on her behalf had helped the most.

"Hello, Iris." Elizabeth smiled at Ferris's receptionist as she greeted her.

"Lissa, dear! How nice to see you!" The petite, gray-haired nurse smiled back and stood up to lean over the partition to grasp Elizabeth's extended hand. "Doctor has someone with him right now," Iris then said, "but he'll be with you in a few minutes. Now tell me all about your travels in Europe. You must really have enjoyed yourself to stay away so long."

Elizabeth immediately felt guilty at having to back up the fiction that, after the strain of her father's illness and death, she had taken off for Europe for a year to heal her battered emotions. Only Ferris Cabot knew the truth about what she'd really been doing, but she trusted him completely to keep the truth to himself.

"Oh, there's so much to see and do in Europe," Elizabeth said awkwardly, "I hardly know where to start."

Elizabeth breathed a sigh of relief when a buzzer sounded, signaling Iris that Ferris wanted to talk to her.

Saved by the bell, she thought wryly.

"Yes, Doctor," Iris said over the phone, then hung up and smiled at Elizabeth. "He wants you to come into his office, dear. You know the way."

Elizabeth smiled back. "I ought to," she said teasingly. "I've spent some of my best and my worst times there."

She was referring to the fact that Ferris was not only her godfather, and as such had been delighted to talk to Elizabeth about medicine when he could spare the time, but that he had been her pediatrician as well, dispensing examinations, shots, and treatment when she needed them.

Ferris's office door was open, and she could see him sitting behind his familiar desk reading a medical journal and talking to himself out loud. And suddenly, she was so glad to be with someone whom she knew cared about her personally, as well as her ambition to be a doctor, that she rushed into the room, swept behind his desk, and threw her arms around his neck.

"Uncle Ferris, you darling!" she exclaimed with spontaneous affection. "It's so good to be back here with you."

Ferris started chuckling as he put down his journal. "Whoa," he said with mock gruffness. "Don't strangle me, girl!"

An instant later, he was on his feet giving Elizabeth a proper hug, then he held her away from him and looked her over.

Elizabeth's natural taste in clothes was conservative, and she was wearing a wool charcoal-gray tailored jacket, a white silk blouse with a red-and-black silk scarf loosely knotted at the neck, a pale gray straight skirt, black pumps, and silver earrings and bracelet.

Now that she no longer had to wear wigs, she intended to let her hair grow long, but meanwhile it formed a black, loosely curled halo around her delicately carved features.

"You're as beautiful as ever," Ferris said fondly. "More so, in fact. The last couple of years have put something new in those lovely violet eyes of yours. You're not a little girl anymore."

Elizabeth grinned, showing her even white teeth. "I haven't been a little girl for longer than two years, Uncle Ferris," she teased him, "but thanks for the compliment. It's nice to be able to be my—"

Some small sound behind her made Elizabeth break off and turn her head in the direction of the bookcases that lined the back wall of Ferris's office. And what she saw there—or rather the person she saw there—drained the color from her smooth complexion, made her large violet eyes widen with incredulity, and kept her mouth open in an expression of shocked disbelief.

"I'm sorry, Lissa," Ferris said smoothly, a pleased expression on his face as he saw that his goddaughter—and his fellow physician and friend, judging by the open pleasure in Sonny Strotherton's blue eyes as he stared at Elizabeth—were obviously making an impression on one another. Ferris was pleased that he'd had the idea of introducing these two.

"This is Dr. Sonny Strotherton, an internist friend of mine," Ferris performed the introductions. "Sonny, this is Elizabeth Farrell, my goddaughter, former patient, and soon-to-be medical student at Harvard."

Sonny inclined his head. "I'm very pleased to meet you, Ms. Farrell," he said. He wondered whether he should be flattered that she was staring at him as though she couldn't believe her eyes—and very lovely eyes they were, too . . . in fact there was something vaguely familiar about them—or whether his ego was about to receive an unaccustomed jolt. He hoped he was making as good an impression on Elizabeth Farrell as she was making on him. She was the best-looking woman he'd met in a very long time . . . possibly ever.

Elizabeth's mind was boiling with horror at this turn of events. Somehow, she managed to mumble a similar polite greeting in a faint voice, but she was secretly steeling herself to hear Sonny Strotherton say something like, "You look familiar to me, Ms. Farrell. Haven't we met before?"

"I hope you don't mind, Lissa," Ferris was saying, and Elizabeth forced herself to turn her attention to him, though she could barely focus on his words. "But I invited Sonny to join us for lunch. He and I are working on a paper together concerning the differences in juvenile and adult mononucleosis, and between our two busy schedules, we seldom have time to get together as often as we'd like."

Elizabeth swallowed against the panic clogging her throat. "No, I don't mind, Uncle Ferris," she said weakly. "In fact, if you and Dr. . . . Sto . . . ah, Stro . . ."

"Call me Sonny," Sonny broke in, giving her a charming smile while he wondered whether it was something about him that was making Elizabeth Farrell stutter, or whether she had a speech impediment.

Elizabeth managed to nod, and quickly turned her eyes away from Sonny Strotherton's handsome—and altogether too familiar—face to look at her Uncle Ferris again.

"What I mean to say is," she forced herself to speak more slowly, "if you two would like to have lunch alone, I don't mind in the least. I have so many things to do to get ready for the spring semester anyway that—"

"Don't be silly!" Ferris Cabot scoffed, taking her arm to guide her toward the door while he gestured at Sonny with his other hand. "What two men with any sense would forgo your delightful company?"

"Certainly not I," Sonny said smoothly, meaning it, as he put the medical book he'd been thumbing through back into the bookcase and came to join the other two at the door. "I'd much prefer to look at you across the table, Ms. Farrell, than at Ferris."

Ferris laughed heartily, and as Elizabeth glanced up at the pleased look on her godfather's face, it finally dawned on her that he had set this whole thing up deliberately. Her misguided godfather was doing a little matchmaking, God forbid!

"Call her 'Lissa,' Sonny," Ferris invited on Elizabeth's behalf, much to her dismay. "All of us who are close to her use her nickname, and I'm sure the two of you are going to become fast friends."

Elizabeth involuntarily met Sonny's gaze, and she felt a weak sensation quaver through her as she saw that his expression was warmly amused. He raised his brows at her, silently asking her permission to use her nickname rather than taking Ferris's invitation at face value.

"Ah . . . yes, of course," she managed to get out in an approximation of her normal voice. "Call me Lissa."

"Thank you, Lissa," Sonny replied in a tone as warm as his look. He was growing more enchanted by the beautiful Lissa Farrell by the moment. After less than five minutes in her company, he was already making plans to ask her out, and without any of the uncertainty he usually felt when meeting a new woman.

"Come along, you two," Ferris said, pulling Elizabeth through the door of his office. "I have to be back for appointments by two, so we'd better be on our way."

In an agony of nervous apprehension, Elizabeth allowed her godfather to pull her out of his office, down the hall, and out into the lobby.

"I'll be back in an hour or so, Iris," Ferris informed his receptionist/nurse.

"Yes, Doctor," Iris replied, her shrewd eyes flitting between Elizabeth and Sonny speculatively.

Outside the building, Ferris opened the front passenger door of his gray Mercedes for Elizabeth, and though she would much have preferred to sit in the back rather than be put on view for Sonny Strotherton, there wasn't much point in protesting, so she climbed in and sat stiffly facing forward while Sonny got in the backseat and Ferris came around to get in the driver's seat.

"I thought we'd go to a new little French restaurant that's just opened nearby," Ferris said smoothly as he started the car. "You can let us know how it compares with the real thing in Paris, Lissa," he added, letting her know that he hadn't let Sonny Strotherton in on her secret.

His words would have made Elizabeth relax if she'd had no previous contact with Sonny, but as it was, she wasn't reassured that the makeup and costume she'd worn as the Vixen had been good enough to prevent Sonny from tumbling at some point to the fact that Elizabeth Farrell and the Vixen were one and the same.

She merely gave Ferris a faint smile instead of answering, but Sonny spoke up and she was faced with telling an out-and-out lie, something she abhorred doing.

"Oh, have you traveled abroad extensively then, Lissa?" he asked.

Elizabeth cleared her throat, but fortunately, Ferris answered for her in a more skillful way than she could have managed herself.

"Lissa's father was Daniel Farrell, the noted pediatrician, Sonny. Did you ever meet him?"

"No, I never had the pleasure," Sonny said gently, "but I'm well-aware of the excellent reputation he had."

Elizabeth involuntarily softened a little at Sonny's tone of voice, which she knew was for her benefit, and his praise of her father.

"Well, Lissa nursed him through his last year," Ferris explained quietly, "and after we lost him, she needed to get away for a while."

Elizabeth glanced at Ferris gratefully when Sonny murmured, "I see," and dropped the subject of her fictitious European travels.

They arrived at the restaurant then, which was reassuringly unpretentious, and when the three of them were seated at a table and were looking at menus, Elizabeth couldn't help peeking over the top of hers for a closer look at Sonny. She had avoided focusing on him too closely when he might have looked back at her.

He was as devastatingly handsome as she remembered, and as her gaze drifted to his well-formed mouth, which was both masculinely sexy and somehow endearingly vulnerable as well, she felt a flood of heat suffuse her as she recalled the kiss they'd shared in her dressing room.

At that instant, Sonny glanced up from his menu, and as Elizabeth hastily raised her gaze from his mouth to the clear ice-blue of his eyes for a second before she glanced back down at her own menu, she could feel an uncontrollable blush staining her cheeks.

Sonny stared at her a moment, stunned by the shaft of arousal that had filled him when he'd caught Lissa staring at his mouth with that curious look of longing on her beautiful face, and by what he'd seen in her eyes for that split second they'd shared a glance.

He had to force himself to return his gaze to his menu, but he saw nothing of the words printed there for wondering about what was going on inside Lissa Farrell. Was she bold or shy . . . a vulnerable young woman or self-confident sophisticate? he wondered, enchanted further by the paradoxical behavior she was exhibiting.

At his age, after years of marriage, he wasn't sure he wanted to deal with the awkwardness an inexperienced young woman might have in dealing with a full-blown romantic relationship. But on the other hand, it might be rather intriguing to become involved with a woman who could manage to convey innocence while her behavior was maturely satisfying.

"What are you going to have, Lissa?" Ferris looked up from his menu to address her.

Elizabeth hadn't been able to focus on her menu, but she covered the fact by smiling over the top of it at Ferris and suggesting he choose for her.

"You've been here before, so you know what's good," she said a great deal more lightly than she felt.

"Green salad and cheese soufflé for you then, girl," Ferris promptly replied. "As I recall, you've never liked to eat heavily during the day."

"True." Lissa nodded, setting her menu aside and immediately beginning an inspection of the room and the other customers in order to keep her eyes from straying in Sonny's direction, a temptation that dismayed her.

Have some sense, Lissa, she grimly instructed herself. *He may look like the answer to a woman's prayers and kiss like every fantasy lover you've ever had, but he's also exactly the sort of man who'll condemn you on general principles and refuse to take you seriously as a doctor if he ever finds out you were the Vixen . . . in fact, he'll be harder on you than others who think like him might be, because he'll hate knowing you know what happened between him and the Vixen.*

"Do you enjoy symphony music, Lissa?" Sonny intruded on her thoughts.

Incautiously, she met his gaze for an instant before sliding her eyes to a point beyond his right shoulder.

"Yes, I do," she admitted reluctantly, hoping he wasn't on the verge of issuing an invitation.

"You don't sound very positive about it." Sonny smiled at her with more charm than Elizabeth was able to resist. Her gaze somehow became focused on his mouth again.

"It would be strange if she didn't like the symphony," Ferris interjected with a smile. "Her mother was Amanda Phipps, the concert pianist."

Sonny, though he'd lost interest in the subject of music the moment Lissa had begun staring at his mouth again, managed to say, in an unconsciously thickening voice, "Wonderful. I'm impressed."

His words jarred Elizabeth's concentration on the perfection of his lips, and she frowned as she met his gaze.

"I like *all kinds* of music," she said in a coldly repressive way.

Sonny was surprised and confused by her tone. What had he done to set her off, he wondered.

Ferris said, with a slight warning in his tone, "I'm sure Sonny likes other types of music as well, Lissa. Right, Sonny?"

"Sure," Sonny replied, giving a baffled shrug of his shoulders.

Elizabeth felt embarrassed by her overreaction . . . and she wasn't even certain why she had spoken as she had. She was grateful that Ferris then engaged Sonny in a conversation about the paper they were writing together, giving her time to sort out her feelings.

Sheer defensiveness, she decided a moment later. *He sounded like the sort of snob who considers himself so far above the normal run of humanity that he can only enjoy classical music, classical literature and . . . classical women?*

That thought really focused the matter for her and explained her defensiveness. In her dressing room in New York that night several weeks back, she had interpreted Sonny Strotherton's reaction to the Vixen as contemptuous and superior. And while the act she'd put on for his benefit might partially justify such a reaction on his part, it wasn't the reaction of a true gentleman, and it had hurt her.

To Elizabeth, a true gentleman was a man such as her father had been . . . a man who didn't judge people harshly and who treated people with gentle, sensitive consideration whatever their station in life or their pattern of living. The only thing she'd ever known him to be intolerant of in people was deliberate cruelty. And while Sonny Strotherton's somewhat cruel reaction to the Vixen might have been involuntary rather than deliberate, it showed an orientation she couldn't approve of.

Unaware that she was staring critically at Sonny's impressive profile until he turned his head and frowned his puzzlement at the look on her face, Elizabeth flushed at being caught staring and looked away.

Perhaps you shouldn't point a finger at his shortcomings, she thought with dry self-mockery, *when you're not so good at controlling your own reactions.*

During the meal, Elizabeth had no desire to talk and made an effort to concentrate on the conversation between Sonny and Ferris so that she wouldn't have to think about her ambivalent feelings toward Sonny.

For his part, while Sonny kept one part of his mind on his conversation with Ferris, another part of him was thoroughly confused by Lissa Farrell. He still had every intention of asking her out, of course. But he wasn't as certain that his invitation would be accepted as he'd been when he'd caught Lissa staring at his mouth with that hint of smoldering sexuality in her violet gaze.

When they arrived back at Ferris's office and were standing outside his car to say good-bye, Sonny acted on his intention, but not without some trepidation.

"May I drop you somewhere, Lissa?" he asked with warm politeness. "I have my car here," and he gestured toward a sedate, late-model station wagon parked nearby.

Elizabeth hesitated, trapped by her aversion to Boston traffic. She had come to Ferris's office by taxi.

"Go along with him, Lissa," Ferris teased her. "I can vouch for his character."

Strangely, both Elizabeth and Sonny colored at Ferris's words, both thinking of a kiss exchanged in a New York club's dressing room, though, of course, neither of them dreamed their thoughts were running along the same lines.

"Ah . . . all right," Elizabeth agreed with strained graciousness. "Unless it's out of your way?" she hastily grasped at any straw to get out of being alone with Sonny.

Ferris snorted. "He only lives a few blocks from your place, Lissa," he said, "and his office is farther east of there, so you won't be putting him out."

Elizabeth was dismayed to hear that Sonny Strotherton lived near her, and she found herself wishing that her Uncle Ferris wasn't quite so determined to be helpful in keeping her and Sonny together.

"Fine," she said rather stiffly and made herself give Ferris a hug and a kiss on the cheek in a natural manner. "You and Aunt Sarah come to dinner soon, Uncle Ferris. You know you're always welcome."

"We will, honey," Ferris replied. "And we'll try to make it before the spring semester starts. Somehow, knowing you and your study habits, I don't think you'll be interested in having dinner guests after that."

Elizabeth smiled faintly and stood back as Sonny and Ferris shook hands, then stiffened when Sonny took her arm to guide her toward his car. "This way," he said unnecessarily, a smile on his lips because he found touching Lissa Farrell, even through layers of clothing, very pleasing.

Elizabeth forced herself not to pull her arm out of his grip, but she was grateful when they reached his car and he unlocked the door for her. But she found the fact that he held on to her arm until after she was seated in the passenger seat alarming, though not quite so alarming as the fact that, despite her best intentions, she had liked walking close to his tall body and having him hold on to her so protectively . . . or was it *possessively?*

"This spell of warm weather has been nice, hasn't it?" Sonny spoke casually as he pulled out of the parking space and headed for the street. "We'll have more snow and cold soon enough, I expect."

"Yes . . . I expect so," Elizabeth replied stiffly, wishing it weren't so far to her house, wishing Sonny weren't going to learn where she lived as a result of this ride, wishing she weren't so physically drawn to this man.

"I can't believe we've lived in the same city and moved in the same circles all these years without meeting one another," Sonny said, projecting a note into his voice that said he regretted the lapse.

"Oh . . . it happens," Elizabeth replied, wondering what Sonny would say if he ever found out that they had met before, and what the circumstances of those meetings had been.

Sonny glanced over, and seeing a frown on Lissa's lovely face, he gave a silent sigh, wondering what he'd done this time to provoke her.

"Lissa, are you annoyed with me about something?" he tackled the matter head on.

Elizabeth stiffened inside. "Why . . . no . . . of course not," she said. What else could she say without revealing *why* she was annoyed with him and thereby giving herself away?

"Well, good," Sonny said with a trace of dryness in his voice. "I'm not aware of having done anything to make you angry, but one never knows."

Elizabeth suppressed a smile, thinking, *No, one doesn't . . . and I hope you never find out what it is you've done.*

"Back at the restaurant, I had a purpose in mind when I asked you if you liked the symphony," Sonny went on in a warmer tone, making Elizabeth stiffen inside again. When she didn't say anything, Sonny continued speaking. "I have tickets for a concert this weekend. It's being held to raise money for the symphony. Would you like to come with me?"

Yes! Elizabeth's traitorous heart answered silently, followed an instant later by an equally vehement and just as sincere *No!*

"Oh . . . I . . . ah . . . ," she started stumbling for an answer, her mind blank of excuses for the time being.

Sonny glanced at her, his mouth compressing into a tight line as he saw that she was searching for a way to turn him down. Ordinarily, he would have let it go if a woman didn't want to go out with him, though he had seldom been faced with such a reaction to one of his invitations. But there was something about Elizabeth Farrell that wouldn't let him risk rejection. He had to see her again, and that was all there was to it.

A small park lay on their right, and almost without thinking, Sonny pulled the car into a parking space fronting it, while Elizabeth looked at him wide-eyed and puzzled.

"What are you doing?" she asked faintly as Sonny killed the motor, then turned in his seat to look at her.

Sonny answered her indirectly. "Lissa, I've been a widower for two years," he said firmly, holding her gaze when she would dearly have loved to be able to look away. "And during the last year, I've started dating again, though not seriously . . . at least, I haven't met anyone I wanted to date seriously . . . until today."

Elizabeth felt her breath get stuck in her throat, but she couldn't look away and she couldn't speak, for some reason.

"I know we've barely met," Sonny went on more quietly, searching Elizabeth's face for a reaction, "but I think you're one of the most beautiful women I've ever seen. I haven't been able to get my mind on anything else but you since the moment Ferris introduced us. And I would very much like the chance to see more of you," he added, his voice softening to a caress. "Please, Lissa. Will you give me that chance?"

Elizabeth finally managed to take a breath. Then she swallowed and searched for something to say that would reflect her true feelings. But she was so confused about her feelings concerning Sonny Strotherton that nothing came to mind, and her silence prompted Sonny to speak again.

"Come to the concert with me Saturday night, Lissa," he said persuasively as he reached across the seat to wrap one of her dark curls around his finger.

When he tugged at the curl he held very gently, Elizabeth was amazed at the erotic sensations the action provoked inside her. *Good heavens!* she thought with bewildered alarm. Am I *that* drawn to him?

Then he let go of the curl and moved his fingers to her flushed cheek, stroking her smooth skin lightly with the backs of them. Again, Elizabeth experienced a flash of arousal, and her bewilderment grew. He was doing nothing in the least overtly erotic. So why was she reacting as vividly as though he had touched her in a much more intimate fashion?

"I . . ." She stopped and swallowed again. "I'm not sure that would be a good idea," she got out, but her voice sounded unsteady and breathless.

"Why?" Sonny's smile was tender and warm and caressing.

A good question, Elizabeth thought rather frantically. "Well, I'm going to be starting medical school very soon." She attempted to put a degree of firmness into her voice. She failed so blatantly that she became irritated with her own indecisiveness. "I won't have time for much of a social life then," she added, frowning at herself much more than at Sonny.

Sonny's smile widened. "Hey, Lissa," he said softly. "I've been there, remember? I know the demands that will be made on your time. But I also know that no matter how hard you work at your studies, there will always be time left over, and I'd like to spend some of it with you."

Elizabeth blinked at him helplessly. "We've barely met," she protested weakly. "You can't be sure you'll want to keep seeing me . . ."

Sonny merely shrugged, and his smile didn't abate in the slightest, and his eyes, behind which was a growing warmth, were on hers, and then on her mouth, and then back to her eyes, and Elizabeth found herself saying, "All right, I'll go to the concert with you Saturday night."

The smile broadened into a grin then, and despite Elizabeth's dismay at what she'd done, she was captivated by it.

"Thank you, Lissa," Sonny said, bringing one finger down from her cheek to her mouth. He stroked her upper lip just once, dazing Elizabeth in the process, and then he shifted in his seat, started the car, and backed out of the parking space.

Neither of them spoke again until they reached Elizabeth's home.

"I've passed this place many times," Sonny said admiringly, "and I've always liked it. Have you lived here long?"

"All my life," Elizabeth said faintly. She was still dazed by the power of her attraction to Sonny and the danger she was courting in giving in to that attraction, if only for one date.

Then she realized she'd better get out of the car and send Sonny on his way before Danny or Jay or Darla appeared on the scene, provoking the necessity of making some very awkward introductions.

"Thank you for the ride," she said quickly as she reached for the door handle and started to open the door.

"And thank you for agreeing to come out with me," Sonny said smoothly. "I'll pick you up at six thirty on Saturday, if that's all right with you, Lissa."

"But the concerts usually don't start until—"

"We'll have dinner first," Sonny said with such firm confidence that Elizabeth was discouraged from arguing with him.

"All right," she said on a defeated sigh as she pushed her car door open and climbed out. "Thanks again for the ride."

She shut the door before Sonny could reply and walked hurriedly toward the front door of her home, waiting to hear the sound of Sonny backing out of the driveway as she walked.

When she realized he was going to wait until she got inside before he left, she walked faster, and when the front door at last closed behind her, she had the curious sensation of reaching safety from a very real danger on the other side of the door . . . a danger that had little to do with the exposure of her role as the Vixen, and a great deal to do with exposure of her heart to the pain of invasion.

CHAPTER SEVEN

"Who are you going out with?" Maggie Strotherton asked sharply as she sat on the end of her father's bed and watched him struggle with the black tie of his tuxedo.

"You don't know her. She's Dr. Cabot's goddaughter." Sonny answered calmly though he wasn't feeling particularly calm at the moment. Not only was he more nervous about a date than he remembered being since high school, he was annoyed by the familiar signs of possessive curiosity Maggie was exhibiting.

"What's her name?" Maggie almost demanded.

Sonny's annoyance grew, but he kept his voice under control.

"Elizabeth Farrell," he answered. "Her nickname's Lissa."

"You're already calling her by her nickname?" Maggie asked in a suspicious tone.

Sonny finally finished with his tie, gave himself one last look in the mirror, then turned toward his daughter.

"Dr. Cabot introduced her by her nickname, Maggie," he said levelly. "Come on. I'll sit with you while you have your dinner."

"Huh!" Maggie snorted, lifting her tiny nose into the air as she hopped up from the bed and headed for the door. "You don't have to. I wouldn't want to make you late for your *date!*"

Like hell, you wouldn't, Sonny thought, half amused, half angry at Maggie's transparent behavior.

As he followed his daughter's flouncing figure downstairs, Sonny realized that if he and Lissa were headed for the sort of relationship he'd been hoping to find, he and Maggie were probably going to have some major confrontations over the matter. He should have scotched the sort of behavior she was displaying now when it had first surfaced, rather than waiting until it mattered enough to him to call her on it. Since she was probably under the impression her behavior had accomplished her purpose before, she had no reason to change it now.

At the small table in the breakfast nook off the kitchen where Sonny and Maggie normally took their meals—they only used the dining room when they had company—Sonny looked thoughtfully at the sullen expression on his daughter's face and the way she was merely toying with her lamb chops.

"Maggie, let me ask you something," he said in a casual way.

Maggie glanced at him and shrugged by way of answer.

"Suppose I were to tell you you couldn't be friends with Peggy Andrews anymore?"

Peggy Andrews had been Maggie's closest friend since first grade, and her reaction to Sonny's question was wide-eyed shock, but before she could say anything, he went on.

"Or suppose I decided not to allow you to single-date until you're eighteen?"

Now Maggie looked at him with fiery indignation. "You wouldn't do that!" she exclaimed.

"Why wouldn't I?" Sonny asked calmly.

"Well, because . . . ," Maggie sputtered, ". . . because I'd run away or something if you did!"

Sonny raised his eyebrows at her, and Maggie stuck her lower lip out for a moment before she got a thoughtful look in her eyes and gradually started to smile.

"But you wouldn't do it," she said scoffingly.

"I repeat . . . why wouldn't I?" Sonny drawled.

Maggie's look was smugly confident. "Because you love me, Daddy," she said matter-of-factly, "and you know how much Peggy means to me and how much I look forward to being allowed to single-date. You like to give me things I want."

She shrugged, as though the matter were settled.

Sonny nodded, his gaze steady. "And do you love me, Maggie?"

Maggie's smile faded and, as though she sensed a trap, she began to frown.

"Of course I love you, Daddy," she said impatiently.

"Enough to be glad for me when I have something I want?"

The trap sprang shut, and Maggie began scowling thunderously.

"If you're talking about getting married again, it's not the same thing at all!" she snapped.

"No?" Sonny's brows were raised again.

"No, because I'll have to live with your new wife, too, and it's not fair if I don't like her," Maggie spoke rapidly, not allowing Sonny to break in, "and besides, I know what women are like, Daddy!"

"Oh?" Sonny could hardly keep his smile under control, but he managed it. "And what are they like, Maggie?" he asked with nothing more than polite curiosity in his tone.

"They twist men like you around their little fingers," Maggie said sternly, "just so they can get your money and live in a big house like this and be married to a doctor! You have to be careful, Daddy," she said, lifting a finger to shake it at him. "Men are fools for a pretty face and a sexy body! Women can . . ."

"Maggie!" Sonny said exasperatedly, pushing her finger firmly out of his face. "What do you know about . . . Well, never mind! I don't know where you've picked up that kind of cynicism about your own sex, but all women aren't like that by a long shot! Your mother wasn't, and—"

"Of course, *Mom* wasn't!" Maggie interrupted, and now her large blue eyes began to glisten with tears. "Mom was wonderful. That's why I couldn't stand it if you married someone awful."

"Maggie, give me a little credit," Sonny said gently. He wasn't sure whether Maggie's tears were entirely genuine, or a combination of real grief for the loss of her mother and a weapon to keep him in line, but he couldn't risk misjudging her. "I hope I'm wiser than to get involved with someone awful."

For just an instant, a vision of the Vixen flashed across Sonny's mind and provoked a sensation of guilt inside him, but he impatiently pushed the feeling down. After all, he wouldn't marry someone like the Vixen in a million years!

"I doubt it!" Maggie said in a choked voice. "Men don't care what a woman's really like as long as she's pretty and sexy and can make him believe he's smart and handsome and better than other men!"

Sonny sighed. "That's just not true, Maggie," he said gently. "At least, it's not true of me," he added, hoping to God it wasn't. "I wouldn't marry a woman who didn't have a good character to go along with the rest of her."

"Hmph!" was Maggie's sullen comment as she picked up her fork and began to swirl it through her mashed potatoes.

Mrs. Mullins, their housekeeper, came in from the kitchen at that moment, and looked at Maggie's plate in surprise.

"What's the matter, honey?" she asked in concern. "Are you sick, or is there something wrong with the food?"

Maggie glanced at her half defiantly, half guiltily. "No, it's all right," she said grudgingly. "I'm just not hungry. May I be excused, please?" she turned to her father and asked, giving him a stubborn look.

Sonny hesitated, then shrugged. "You may," he said dryly, not seeing the sense of forcing Maggie to eat when she didn't want to.

Maggie promptly pushed her chair back, and without giving Sonny his usual kiss, flounced off toward the stairs to ascend to her room.

Mrs. Mullins looked after her, her kindly face creased with concern.

"Don't worry about her, Mrs. Mullins," Sonny said as he got to his feet. "She's simply upset because I have a date tonight."

Mrs. Mullins immediately brightened. "That's right, you do," she said in a pleased way as she began to gather up Maggie's dishes. "And I hope you have a wonderful time, Dr. Strotherton. It's been too long since you had a chance to enjoy yourself."

Sonny had every intention of enjoying himself, and he was glad Mrs. Mullins, at least, seemed to be on his side, even if his daughter wasn't.

"I wouldn't throw her food away if I were you, Mrs. Mullins," he said, grinning as he headed for the front hall to collect his coat. "If I know my Maggie, she'll be back downstairs in an hour or so, starved for her dinner."

"I wasn't going to, Doctor," Mrs. Mullins responded dryly. "I know our Maggie, too."

Laughing, determinedly putting his problem with Maggie aside for the moment, Sonny headed for an evening he was hoping would be the best few hours he'd spent in over two years.

Elizabeth eyed herself skeptically in the full-length mirror in her bedroom, wondering if she'd overdone it.

She was wearing a black velvet evening outfit consisting of a bolero jacket, a long, full skirt, and a white silk blouse trimmed with multicolored Mexican embroidery. She had a hat that went with the outfit, but not the courage to wear it—at least not tonight—not with Sonny Strotherton, the ultimate stuffed shirt.

She frowned as she realized there was no reason in the world why she should worry one whit whether Sonny Strotherton approved of her appearance or not. This was the first and the last date she intended to have with him, and if she hadn't been such a fool as to fall for his handsome exterior and charming manner, she wouldn't even be going on this one!

"Forewarned is forearmed," she muttered, hoping against hope that her words would stick rather than go flying off into the wind at the first glance she had of Sonny in a tuxedo.

As she grabbed up her evening purse and headed downstairs, Elizabeth counted her blessings that the Foursome had left late that afternoon for an engagement in Philadelphia. Danny had wanted to give Darla a chance to rehearse in the hall where they would be playing tomorrow, and though Darla had been somewhat insulted by his lack of confidence in her, she hadn't said anything except to Lissa.

"I'm going to knock his socks off!" she had whispered to her newfound friend as they left.

Elizabeth had nodded firmly and patted her shoulder in an encouraging manner. "You bet, you will!"

Now, though she was grateful for her luck, Elizabeth couldn't believe she had actually accepted an invitation from Sonny Strotherton without having a plan in mind to keep him from meeting Danny, Jay, and Darla . . . which was another good reason why she had no intention of ever accepting another invitation from Sonny.

Downstairs, she paced the living room in a nervous manner until a sweep of light through the living room alerted her to the fact that Sonny had pulled into the driveway.

"Oh, God!" Elizabeth said out loud on an intake of breath and a sudden upsurge of panic. "Why did you ever say yes, you fool!"

When she opened the door to Sonny a few minutes later, however, she was the picture of calm serenity, an act that cost her a great deal of effort to accomplish.

"Good evening, Sonny," she said lightly. "Come in. I'm ready. Just let me get my coat."

She turned away from the door, leaving Sonny to shut it behind him and moved to the hall closet.

"You look beautiful tonight, Lissa," Sonny said from directly behind her a second later, making Elizabeth jump.

"Oh . . . ah . . . thank you," she said, barely glancing at him over her shoulder. "So do you," she added unconsciously, not even aware of the revealing inappropriateness of her words, though they made Sonny grin.

He didn't respond verbally, however, and he had his grin under control by the time Elizabeth had pulled a long, black cashmere cape from its hanger, and he reached to take it from her.

"Oh . . . thank you," Elizabeth said, holding tightly on to her control.

Sonny couldn't help himself. After placing the cape around Lissa's shoulders, he let his hands rest far longer than necessary on her shoulders as the lovely scent of her hair and perfume filled his nostrils.

"You smell intoxicating," he said, a softly gruff note in his voice.

"I'm glad you like it . . . it's a new perfume I'm trying," Lissa said faintly. She was becoming ever more nervous over Sonny's closeness, and she stepped forward out of his reach. Turning, she attempted a bright smile. "Shall we go?" she suggested, and quickly headed for the door without waiting for Sonny's reply.

As he followed her, Sonny was ruefully aware that he was going to have to take better control of his actions. Obviously, Lissa Farrell was the type of woman who didn't appreciate overly precipitate advances from a man . . . except that they had worked for him in getting her to go to the concert with him, hadn't they?

When they were on the road, he glanced over at Lissa. "I didn't want to take you somewhere where you might not like the food, so I made reservations at a French restaurant," he said. "Next time, you can let me know in advance where you'd like to eat."

Next time? Elizabeth thought, uneasy about his assumption that this was the start of something. As far as she was concerned, there wasn't going to be any "next time," but she didn't say that. Instead, she made herself smile.

"That's fine," she said, then quickly changed the subject. "What is the symphony doing tonight?" she asked brightly.

Sonny smiled. "Ravel." And the gleam in his eyes when he glanced over at her unnerved her.

She forced herself to laugh in a way she hoped sounded lightly amused. "Not *Bolero*, I hope." She shrugged. "I think the movie *10* gave that tune a highly overrated potency." She was lying in her teeth, of course. She found *Bolero* a very effective piece in producing a certain mood . . . but it was a mood she didn't want to feel this particular night.

Sonny merely shrugged. "What would you prefer instead?" he asked.

"Oh . . . ah . . . Mozart has always been one of my favorites," she tossed off without thinking.

Sonny raised his brows as he glanced over at her. "Odd," he murmured, but not loudly enough for Elizabeth to hear. And then louder, he added, "Shall we see what we can find on the radio?" And he reached over to touch a button on the dash.

Immediately, the car was filled with the sound of Elizabeth's voice huskily crooning, "You're the only man for me . . . the *only* man for me . . ."

Elizabeth jerked her eyes to the lighted dial, appalled by what she was hearing. "Oh, please . . . not that!" she said with entirely unthinking fervor.

Sonny was only too happy to snap off the radio. This was definitely not the time he wanted to be reminded of the Vixen and what that song did to him.

"Sorry," he said somewhat grimly into the resulting silence. "I guess my daughter put the radio on that station." Which was probably true, but he didn't add that he had no objection to listening to that particular station—or that particular song—normally.

Elizabeth frantically sought for a way to get off of the subject of music. "You have a daughter?" she quickly asked.

"Yes," Sonny nodded. "Her name's Margaret . . . Maggie for short."

"How nice," Elizabeth encouraged him to go on. "How old is she?"

"Twelve," Sonny almost sighed. "It's rather a difficult age."

Elizabeth was able to laugh more naturally this time. "Yes, I remember," she said sympathetically. "But don't despair. One day, she'll start behaving like a normal human being again."

"I'm not sure she ever did behave like a normal child," Sonny responded ruefully.

Having met Maggie, Elizabeth didn't take him seriously. "Oh, you've just forgotten," she said with a shrug. "I'd be willing to bet she had you completely wrapped around her finger when she was smaller."

Sonny felt startled at Lissa's use of a description Maggie had flung at him earlier that evening.

"Well, I'm certain she'd like to be able to do that now," he responded dryly, "but I'm equally certain it's not in my—or her—best interests to let her get away with it."

Elizabeth laughed, remembering the wonderful relationship she'd shared with her father. Wonderful or not, however, she hadn't been above trying out her newly emerging feminine wiles on him at Maggie's age to get what she wanted. Her father had skillfully parried the attempts, without damaging her confidence in herself. She said as much to Sonny.

"And how did he accomplish such a monumental task?" Sonny asked with dry curiosity.

"Oh, he'd simply hug me and give me lots of compliments and

then good-naturedly stand firm about saying no to me if he thought it was in my best interest."

Sonny nodded thoughtfully. "Sounds like good strategy," he agreed.

"It was . . . though I didn't think so at the time." Elizabeth chuckled.

They arrived at the restaurant, and when they were seated in a rather secluded alcove and had been served their wine, Sonny raised his glass in a toast to Elizabeth.

"To one of the most beautiful women I've ever had the good fortune to meet," he said lightly.

Elizabeth frowned slightly.

"What is it?" Sonny paused with the glass of wine halfway to his lips. "Do you dislike compliments?"

Elizabeth hesitated, then shrugged. "It's not that I dislike compliments," she said quietly, daring to meet Sonny's gaze with her own, briefly. "It's just that I had nothing to do with the way I look. But I've made an effort to cultivate my mind, so I'd really prefer compliments having to do with my intelligence or my character. I feel more comfortable taking at least some credit for them."

Sonny put his glass down, his gaze thoughtful.

"Then I suppose it's premature to compliment you at all," he said with a slight smile, "since I don't know enough about your mental abilities or your character to comment. However," he added, his smile widening when he saw that his words had surprised Lissa, "I think it's unfair to say you can't take any credit at all for your looks. From where I sit, it's obvious that you've taken what you were born with and enhanced it with makeup and a good haircut and wonderful taste in clothes." He shrugged, his eyes mocking Elizabeth. "So I repeat . . . to one of the most beautiful women it has ever been my good fortune to meet."

He slowly and deliberately raised his glass to his mouth, holding Elizabeth's gaze all the while, and drank the whole thing off.

Though she was as fascinated with Sonny's looks as he seemed to be with hers, Elizabeth wasn't fooled that such a basis for a relationship had any validity. Without commenting on her thoughts, however, she lowered her lashes over her eyes and took a brief sip of her wine, then was grateful that the waiter approached and flourished menus at them, providing a welcome diversion.

She chose a small filet mignon with a wine sauce, baked potato, and green salad. Sonny ordered fish. Then the waiter was gone, and Sonny was staring across the table at Lissa. He was seized with a strong desire to get them to a comfortable stage so they could begin to get to know one another.

"Lissa," he addressed her quietly, "I'll ask you again. Is there something about me you don't like?"

Startled by the question, Elizabeth focused on the expression in his blue eyes, which was a mistake because the expression was so warm and approving of her that she couldn't possibly answer him as discouragingly as she knew she should. But perhaps she could be a little more honest than she'd ever been so far in their brief acquaintance?

"Sonny, it would be hard for anyone to dislike you," she said, a dryly teasing note in her voice.

"Well, that's encouraging," he responded in the same manner, but there was still a question in his eyes.

Elizabeth sighed, and her expression sobered as she leaned toward him, her eyes on his. "But Sonny, I wonder if you aren't just a little . . . well, snobbish?"

Sonny was startled. "Snobbish?" he echoed blankly.

Elizabeth sighed again, searching for the right words. Then they came to her, and her gaze was searching as she said them.

"Suppose I didn't dress conservatively, wore more makeup, lived in a shabby neighborhood and had a more flamboyant career in mind than becoming a pediatrician?" she asked. "Would I still be sitting across from you in this expensive restaurant, preparing to accompany you to a symphony concert?"

Sonny took his time, thinking the question over carefully before answering.

"Perhaps you would," he finally said soberly, "but my objective in asking you out would probably be different than it is."

Elizabeth was reluctant to ask the obvious question, but she couldn't stop herself.

"And what is your objective in asking me out?" she said faintly. "And what would it be if I were different . . . more like the woman I just described?"

"My objective in asking out your fictitious woman . . . although I probably wouldn't want to ask her out at all," Sonny replied honestly, "would be a reluctant fascination with her sex appeal. My objective in asking you out, Lissa, is, hopefully, to begin a full-blown *relationship.*"

Before Elizabeth could respond, if indeed she could have come up with anything to say, Sonny went on.

"Now, it's my turn," he said with a wry inflection in his voice. "Suppose that instead of being a respectable doctor with a fairly high income, a house in a decent neighborhood, and the sort of manners expected of a man in my position, I were the male equivalent of the woman you described. Would you be sitting across from me in this expensive restaurant, preparing to go to a symphony concert with me?"

Elizabeth stared at him, trying to be objective. He had a point, but he was missing the real basis of her question.

"It would depend entirely on the sort of man you were beneath the flamboyant career, clothing, and behavior," she answered quietly.

Sonny straightened, everything in him alerted to the importance of what he was about to hear.

"And what sort of man would that be?" he asked intently.

Without hesitating, Elizabeth answered, "A kind man, a decent man, a man tolerant and forgiving of his fellow humans, a man dedicated to make the best of whatever talents he had."

Sonny relaxed slightly. As far as he knew, he met all of the criteria Lissa had described.

"And I would describe a woman I could relate to much in the same terms," he said. "But I can't help it if I would also like her taste in clothes and makeup and leisure activities to run along the same lines as mine."

Elizabeth wished they hadn't started this conversation. She understood the validity of Sonny's view. Everyone had certain tastes, and was naturally inclined to be more comfortable with people whose tastes were similar. But that logical deduction didn't erase the hurt she'd felt in her dressing room the night Sonny had kissed her in her role as the Vixen and she'd seen the look on his face that held her in contempt.

"Lissa?" Sonny called her back from her thoughts, his expression puzzled. "What are you thinking?"

Elizabeth raised her head and looked him straight in the eye.

"Oh, I was just thinking that this conversation is really academic," she said coolly, "because it will be a long time before I'm in a position to become emotionally involved with any man."

Sonny felt as though he'd been kicked in the stomach, and Elizabeth saw his reaction in his face. But now that she'd started, she felt she had to make her position clear. Though Sonny Strotherton might, or might not, deserve the kind of disappointment she was dealing him, it was only fair to stop him from weaving fantasies about deepening their relationship.

"When I am ready to fall in love," she said clearly and distinctly, "I have no doubt that I will recognize the right man when he comes along. I'm only grateful that I haven't met him yet . . . because this isn't the right time."

As Elizabeth watched Sonny absorb her meaning and react to it, she wondered why she felt bleakly unhappy about what she was doing, rather than confident that she was doing the right thing.

But her unhappiness dissolved into alarm as she saw that, after his first reaction of crushing disappointment, Sonny Strotherton was recouping his confidence. In fact, it seemed that, far from discouraging him entirely, her words had goaded him as though she'd issued a challenge.

His next words confirmed this.

"It seems to me," Sonny tossed off with a casualness belied by the gleam of determination in his eyes, "that one should never be too adamant about whom one will love . . . or when. Fate has a way of making us mortals eat our words."

And with that, he picked up the bottle of wine and refilled Elizabeth's glass and his own, then leaned back in his chair to savor the vintage slowly and with pleasure . . . almost as much pleasure as he was deriving from the look of panic in Lissa's widened violet eyes.

CHAPTER EIGHT

Elizabeth paid little attention to the concert. It merely served as background music for her thoughts, which were decidedly chaotic.

She tried to be grateful that after their initial talk, Sonny had steered the conversation away from personal matters and had set himself out to entertain her, which he had. But she had the strangest feeling that he was merely filling time before going on the attack again. And if that was true, she'd have given a lot to be able to predict what form that attack would take.

I can handle anything he dishes out, she tried to bolster her courage. Except there was a condition to her mental statement, and she was aware of what it was. No doubt she could handle anything Sonny might *say* to undermine her determination not to get involved with him. It was what he might *do* that worried her. When she let herself, she remembered all too vividly what she had felt when he'd kissed her, and she didn't exactly trust her ability to discount such feelings.

The thunder of applause signaling the end of the concert made Elizabeth jump in her seat. Then she recovered her equilibrium and joined in, hoping Sonny hadn't noticed how preoccupied she'd been all evening.

Sonny had very definitely noticed Lissa's preoccupation that evening and had found her state of mind reassuring. If he had really made no impression on her, wouldn't her mind have been free to focus on the concert?

Actually, there were other nebulous things about her behavior that bolstered his confidence, but nothing he could put his finger on. He only knew that her attempt to discourage him had somehow rung hollow, and he was inclined to trust his gut feeling that Lissa Farrell was very definitely attracted to him. It only remained to discover why she didn't want to act on that attraction.

"Would you like to go somewhere for a drink?" he asked her as they came out into the crisp night air.

"Oh . . . ah . . . no. . . ." Elizabeth shook her head, wishing she could find her normal decisive manner wherever she'd lost it since meeting Sonny Strotherton. "I have a lot of things to do tomorrow, so I'd better get home to bed."

"Are your Sundays always so busy?" he inquired, rather dryly it seemed to Elizabeth.

"Mmm . . . sometimes," she answered, squirming mentally at being forced to skirt the truth so often where Sonny was concerned. It was irritating!

"That's too bad," he said calmly as he escorted her to his car. "I was hoping you could come to dinner at my place tomorrow evening. My daughter would like to meet you." *And no doubt embarrass the dickens out of you in the process,* Sonny added silently with grim humor.

"Oh . . . well . . . not tomorrow, I'm afraid." *What do you mean, not tomorrow?* Elizabeth asked herself irritably. *Not ever! And what does he mean asking you out again anyway after that discussion you had earlier?*

"Some other time, then," Sonny said smoothly and bent to open the car door for her.

Elizabeth glared at the back of his head, wondering what it was going to take to discourage the man! He must have an ego the size of Mount Rushmore!

She quickly cleared her expression as Sonny straightened up. Then she moved her lips into a half-guilty smile before climbing into the car.

It's almost over, she reassured herself as Sonny went around to the other side. *Just hold on for another half hour, and with a little luck and a lot of willpower, you won't ever have to see Sonny Strotherton again.*

There was a brief silence between them as Sonny dealt with traffic and got onto the road home, then he broke it.

"So you're Ferris Cabot's goddaughter," he said thoughtfully. "Was he your physician when you were younger?"

"Yes," Elizabeth answered, relieved that he was going to continue to keep the conversation on relatively impersonal topics.

"He's my daughter Maggie's physician as well," Sonny said.

"You couldn't do better," Elizabeth volunteered. "He was always wonderful to me. I think he purposely scheduled longer than normal appointments with me so we could talk about medicine together." She glanced at Sonny curiously. "Does Maggie have any interest in medicine?"

"I'm not sure what interests Maggie other than music and the strange groups who perform it these days," Sonny said with a shake of his head.

Elizabeth immediately froze for an instant, then decided to get the conversation onto safer topics.

"Well, she's young," she said hastily. "It takes some people longer than others to find their niche in life. I knew what I wanted to do from about the age of nine, but I consider myself lucky to have been so certain."

Sonny glanced over at her, his expression warm. "What's unusual is that you never changed your mind," he said approvingly, "but that probably had a lot to do with your father's influence. I understand he was very special." He paused for a moment, then added, "But, of course, you might just as well have been drawn to a musical career, considering who your mother was. By the way, do you have any brothers or sisters?"

Elizabeth squirmed in momentary panic, but managed to answer in a reasonably normal voice.

"One brother."

"And what does he do?"

Silence.

After a moment, Sonny looked at her again. "Lissa?"

"What?" she answered vaguely, desperately hoping she was going to get through this conversation merely playing it by ear. "I'm sorry," she added quickly. "I was distracted thinking about that paper you and Uncle Ferris are working on together. Didn't I hear recently that there has been an outbreak of adult mononucleosis that takes a different, more debilitating form than is usual in adolescents?"

Puzzled by Lissa's abrupt change of subject, Sonny nevertheless answered her question in the affirmative and then, warming to the subject, went on with more details about the article he and Ferris were writing.

By the time he finished, they had arrived at Elizabeth's darkened home, and she was congratulating herself on having made it through the evening without making any major slips.

As Sonny brought the car to a stop in the driveway, she quickly put her hand on the door release, and half turned to Sonny at the same time.

"Thank you for a lovely evening, Sonny," she said more rapidly than was strictly polite. "I enjoyed it." Which was the biggest lie she'd told all evening. "You needn't walk me to the door. I . . ."

"Of course I'll walk you to your door, Lissa," Sonny interrupted in a firm tone as he switched off the car engine. "Your house is dark. I'll come in with you to make sure it's safe."

"But . . . ," Elizabeth started to protest, but Sonny was already climbing out his door, and by the time he reached her side of the car, she was resigned to allowing him to play the gentleman.

He took her arm as they walked up the sidewalk to the front door, which didn't help to steady her overwrought nerves, then took her key from her, opened the door, reached a hand inside to turn on the light, then handed the key back to her before they entered the house.

"I'm sure everything is fine," Elizabeth said in a strained tone when they were just inside the door. "I don't hear anything, and anyway, we've never had trouble with burglars in this house."

"There's always a first time." Sonny refused to be dissuaded and after closing the door behind Elizabeth, he started off to make an inspection tour.

Elizabeth followed him, trying to remember if there was anything lying around that might provoke awkward questions should Sonny see it. As far as she knew, downstairs, there was only the grand piano in the music room that had belonged to her mother and was now Danny's. Upstairs was a different story, however, and Elizabeth blanched as she remembered the poster of the Freaky Foursome on the wall in Jay's room, as well as the sheets of music paper scattered all over Danny's.

When Sonny eventually arrived at the base of the staircase, Elizabeth was in a state of near panic, and she hastily slid between him and the stairs.

"Really, Sonny, this isn't necessary," she said, and now there was a definite quaver in her voice. "Please . . . just go home, all right?"

She blushed at the rudeness of her suggestion, as well as the edge that had been in her voice when she'd made it. Sonny's brows were up again, which she was beginning to realize meant that he was very curious . . . and perhaps suspicious?

"I'm sorry, Sonny," she said, projecting more weariness in her tone than she actually felt. "I'm just very tired. It's been quite a while since I graduated from college, and I've been putting myself through a refresher course on all the things I'll need to know for medical school, so if you don't mind . . ."

But Sonny was staring at her mouth in a way that made prickles of alarm run down Elizabeth's spine, and she wondered if he'd heard a word she'd said.

"You don't look tired, Lissa," he said softly, moving closer to rest his hands on her waist. Elizabeth couldn't back away because her heels were up against the bottom step of the staircase. "You look absolutely lovely," he added, and now his mouth was coming closer to hers.

Elizabeth stood there, wracked by a combination of panic and enthrallment. Sonny's eyes held hers now, and somehow she'd gotten trapped in that clear blue gaze to the point where she was frozen to the spot. And as his mouth came closer, the male scent of him washed over her and added to her state of enthrallment.

"Lissa . . . ," he whispered a breath away from her lips. "I've never wanted to kiss a woman so much in my life as I want to kiss you right now."

At that, memory assaulted Elizabeth and her eyes widened into an expression of indignant shock, but it was too late. The instant the last word left Sonny's mouth, he closed the distance between them and joined them in a kiss that fairly seared Elizabeth's lips. It seared her memory, as well, cauterizing the wound Sonny had inflicted by reminding Elizabeth of the other kiss they'd shared. And this kiss had every bit as electric an effect on her.

Sonny's arms enfolded her, and since he'd opened his tuxedo jacket at some point, there was only his shirt and the thin material of Elizabeth's blouse between them . . . an ineffective barrier to the warmth of their upper bodies. Elizabeth suddenly felt as though she were being wrapped into a protective yet sense-riveting haven that was both safe and scorching.

As Sonny's mouth moved over hers, gently parting her lips to receive his tongue, she stayed frozen in an inner battle with her willpower. Her body was all too eager to participate in Sonny's lovemaking. Her mind was trying with ever-decreasing effectiveness to talk her into behaving sensibly.

Then Sonny's right hand moved lower to Elizabeth's left hip, pressing her with gentle firmness against the rising heat in his loins, and her mind abruptly lost the battle as her body caught fire from the contact. With complete spontaneity, she circled Sonny's neck with her arms and leaned into him as she opened her mouth wider under his and met the thrust of his tongue with the welcome of her own.

In answer to the spontaneous signal she'd given him, Elizabeth felt a brief shudder move through Sonny's body and heard him make a stifled sound in his throat before he pulled her even tighter against him and his kiss became a great deal more demanding.

The rhythm of Elizabeth's heart increased and her body felt weightless and melting against the heat and muted strength of Sonny's, while her senses came glowingly to life as though ignited into birth by the power of Sonny's reaction to her.

"Lissa . . . Lissa," her name was a thickened caress coming from Sonny's throat as he moved his lips back and forth against hers, moistening her mouth with his tongue before beginning another deep kiss that completed Elizabeth's absorption in the wonder of what was happening.

She was a willing partner in the lovemaking now. Her mouth didn't just follow Sonny's lead, but provoked action . . . her hands were thrust into the thickness of his hair on the back of his neck, guiding him as much as Sonny led . . . her body thrust tantalizingly of its own will against the pressure of his, yet allowed the molding of his hands as though helpless to resist.

"Lissa, let me love you," Sonny grated huskily during the infinitesimal interval between one kiss and another. "God, you don't know how much I want this . . ."

During the kiss that followed his last words, Elizabeth groggily fought for the clarity of mind to answer his plea. As involved as she was in the power of the physical reaction Sonny had provoked in her, a thin line of common sense remained to caution her not to be guided by the lusts of her body. Sonny unknowingly strengthened the thread by ceasing his unrelenting assault on her mouth.

"Lissa, please, darling . . . ," he murmured thickly as he kissed the corners of her mouth, then her cheeks, her eyes, her throat. "Don't send me away. I'm past thought . . . past sense. I want you so badly—"

When he would have seized her mouth again, Elizabeth barely had the strength to turn her head away lest she get caught again in the trap of unthinking response.

"I want you, Sonny . . . ," she admitted on a weak gasp as Sonny's lips seared the tender underside of her jaw. ". . . but . . ."

Sonny's fevered kisses stilled, and he raised a hand to turn Elizabeth's cheek so that she was forced to look into his eyes.

"You can't mean it . . . ," he whispered through a groan of disbelief. "You have to feel as strongly about this as I do."

Elizabeth blinked at him hazily through the fog of her arousal. His words and tone had touched her heart, and the look of almost tortured desire in his eyes was almost impossibly hard to disappoint.

Opening her eyes wider in an unconscious plea, she murmured, "Sonny, it's too soon?" She was somehow unsurprised when the protest came out as a question rather than a statement.

And then she went still as she saw that Sonny was staring into her eyes with an expression of puzzlement, as though he were trying to place something in his mind.

It couldn't have been more clear to Elizabeth what he was trying to sort out if he'd thundered the words into her ear.

Acting on complete instinct, Elizabeth immediately lowered her eyelids and turned her head away at the same moment as she moved her hands to press against Sonny's shoulders. She would have stepped back if there had been room.

"Sonny, you must go," she said shakenly and attempted to move sideways out of his arms.

"Lissa, wait!" In an automatic desire to persuade Lissa to let him love her, Sonny's mind immediately switched from the attempt to place where he'd seen eyes like Lissa's before, to the more immediate problem he faced. "We can't let this end like this."

Elizabeth moved her hands down to Sonny's, which were holding her waist. "Let me go, Sonny," she said with quiet firmness, still with her head down. "I'm not ready for this."

Instead of letting her go, Sonny enfolded her in his arms again with gentle firmness, but he didn't attempt to kiss her. He merely rested his cheek against her hair.

"I don't understand, Lissa," he said softly. "I know what you were feeling . . . you wanted me as much as I want you. You admitted it."

Elizabeth felt wracked by the decision Sonny was forcing her to make. Why did he have to come into her life again right now, she wondered bitterly. And why was she so certain that if he knew the truth about the role she'd once played, he was the one who would be attempting to end this episode between them?

"But I can't allow myself to be sidetracked right now, Sonny. I explained that to you!" she said a little desperately as she gently pushed at his shoulders to make him let her go. "I just can't, Sonny. Please understand."

But Sonny didn't understand. After all, he and Caroline had been married while he was going through medical school. It wasn't easy, but it certainly wasn't impossible to combine love and the preparation for a medical career!

He attempted to make her look at him again, but Lissa wouldn't meet his eyes. "Lissa, this doesn't make sense," he said firmly. "I've been there, remember?"

"But you're a man," she said quickly. "It's easier for a man."

Sonny frowned impatiently. "Perhaps at one time, but not now, Lissa," he objected. "The old prejudices aren't as strong as they used to be. And you have advantages that other women may not have, don't you? You don't keep this place up by yourself, do you?"

He moved away from her enough to gesture at the house, and Elizabeth immediately freed herself from his grasp altogether, turned her back and started walking toward the living room.

Sonny watched her without attempting to follow for a moment, his expression baffled and increasingly stormy. He was stumped for the time being. How was a man supposed to react to a woman who kissed him with all the fervor he could want, then backed off?

The only thing Sonny was absolutely positive about was that he had no intention of backing off himself. He couldn't. Lissa was the woman he'd been waiting for since he'd lost Caroline, even if he hadn't known consciously what he was doing, and now that he'd found her, he wasn't about to lose her.

He followed her to the living room, firming his jaw when he saw that she was waiting by the front door, obviously intending that he leave right away. He approached her and stood in front of her with his hands on his hips.

"Lissa," he said with quiet firmness, "I don't pretend to know what to make of the contradictions in your behavior tonight, but I'll tell you something, and I mean it like I've never meant anything before . . ."

Elizabeth lifted her head to give him one brief, wary glance before she turned her eyes away again.

"There's something pulling us together, Lissa," Sonny said with quiet fervor. "Something special. Something that's rare enough, no one but a fool would ignore it. And I don't think you're a fool, Lissa," Sonny added less fervently. "I think you feel what I feel . . . want what I want. And for that reason, I can't walk away from you the way you're pretending you want me to . . ."

"I'm not pretending!" Elizabeth quickly raised her head and spoke up.

But the anxious look in her eyes, the lack of total conviction in her voice, the fact that she was twisting her hands together in an outward expression of the conflicting emotions that rode her, convinced Sonny that he was right.

"Lissa . . ." He shook his head with frustration. Then his expression firmed, and his eyes were steady as he said, "It isn't going to work, Lissa. I can't let you do this. There's too much potential for the two of us to have . . . everything we want."

Elizabeth wanted to rage at him for his arrogant dismissal of her wishes. Except that she knew she was giving him conflicting signals. She wanted to plead with him to accept her decision not to see him again without having to explain the reasons behind that decision. Except that every time she looked at him, her resolve wavered. And as he reached out a hand to her, she knew that if he touched her again, her resolve would collapse altogether.

"Don't, Sonny!" she said on a half-groan of protest as she stepped back away from his uplifted hand.

She knew an instant later that her behavior had been too revealing once again. Sonny's warm, understanding smile told her so. And then he closed the distance between them, and he caught her face between his hands and searched her eyes for an affirmation of the truth he already knew.

The only defense Elizabeth had was to close her eyes. But when she did, Sonny gently kissed the lids. Then he closed his mouth over hers and slowly, expertly coaxed the reaction he wanted from her.

When the kiss was over, Elizabeth was unable to keep from opening her eyes to stare helplessly at him, knowing as she did so that he was seeing exactly what he wanted to see in her clouded gaze.

"You can't pretend anymore, darling," he murmured with gentle amusement in his deep voice. "And take my advice. Don't ever try to play poker with eyes like that. You'll lose everything in no time."

He kissed her cheek, then let her go and moved to put his hand on the doorknob. "I'll call you tomorrow, Lissa," he said with quiet confidence, "and let you know what time I'm picking you up for dinner."

And before Elizabeth could utter another halfhearted protest, he was through the door and gone, leaving her to stare after him with resentful bewilderment.

CHAPTER NINE

The next morning, Elizabeth woke feeling irritable with herself for letting things go as far with Sonny as they had.

Why is it that men think they have a right to run my life to their satisfaction instead of my own? she asked herself half angrily as she dressed for church. *First Danny sidetracks me and now Sonny wants to do the same!*

After her first cup of coffee, however, she calmed down a little and admitted to herself that it wasn't Sonny's intention to steer her away from medical school . . . he simply wanted her to let him into her life. And she could hardly blame him for dismissing her words about not wanting to get involved with him when her actions had told him exactly the opposite.

She frowned as she recalled how vivid her physical reaction to Sonny had been both times he'd kissed her. Even thinking about it sent a flush of heat through her body. But that was nothing to base a relationship on! Especially when she was positive that Sonny wasn't the sort of person who would regard her brief career as the Vixen with equanimity. He was, in fact, exactly the type of physician she'd had in mind when she'd decided it would be wise to keep her role as the Vixen a secret from the medical community.

As she drove to church a while later, Elizabeth found herself becoming more and more indignant over the necessity for such subterfuge. She knew the Foursome's musical talents—especially Danny's— to be on a par with any symphony orchestra. Yet because they preferred to perform ballads and soft rock rather than classical music, their musical credentials weren't considered legitimate.

And it wasn't just the act I put on in my dressing room that night that made Sonny think of the Vixen as little better than a tramp, she thought grimly. *He disapproves of the Vixen on principle because she doesn't sing opera and dresses outlandishly. And since he feels that way, I can't imagine why he came backstage to see me in the first place!*

The church service soothed her temper, but on the drive back home, Elizabeth faced the fact that no matter what Sonny Strotherton made her feel when he kissed her, they had nothing more going for them than physical attraction to make it worthwhile to see more of him.

"I'll go to dinner with him tonight, all right," she muttered to herself irritably, "but when the evening's over, I'll make things clearer to him than I obviously managed to do last night and end this thing once and for all!"

Sonny took Mrs. Mullins aside before he and Maggie left for church and informed her that Lissa was coming to dinner and that he wanted it to be special.

Mrs. Mullins gave him a wryly amused look. "I'll do my best for you, Doctor," she said, "but if you really want the evening to be special, perhaps you ought to send Maggie over to a friend's house for dinner."

Sonny's smile said he was ruefully aware of the problem. "She does have a way of putting a damper on things, doesn't she," he acknowledged, "and I'm aware she thinks it's worked for her before. But this time, she's going to have to learn to adjust, Mrs. Mullins," he said confidently. "Lissa Farrell is different."

Mrs. Mullins gave him a skeptical look, then shrugged. "I hope you're right, Doctor," she said doubtfully, then went to the freezer to see what there was to cook for a special dinner.

On the drive to church, Sonny matter-of-factly informed Maggie that Lissa was coming to dinner that night.

Predictably, Maggie stiffened up and opened her mouth to voice a protest. But then she seemed to think better of it, and Sonny noticed a sly, fleeting little smile cross his daughter's lips.

"All right, Daddy," she said with suspicious agreeableness and turned away to look out the car window.

"Maggie," Sonny said dryly, "I'm not going to tolerate any rudeness from you tonight, is that understood?"

Maggie turned wide, innocent blue eyes in her father's direction. "Of course, Daddy," she said as though she couldn't understand why he would even bring up the possibility. "I know how to behave."

Sonny was well aware of the duplicity of Maggie's statement, but he didn't challenge her over it for the moment. He would show her when the time came that he meant what he'd said.

After lunch, he conferred with Mrs. Mullins, then went into his study to call Lissa.

"Hello," Elizabeth answered the phone calmly, certain it was Sonny.

"Lissa, this is Sonny," he said, unconsciously using a caressing tone. "Is six o'clock tonight all right? Tomorrow is a school day for Maggie."

"Six is fine for me, Sonny," Elizabeth answered pleasantly, "because I have to make an early night of it myself."

Sonny frowned. "You do?"

"Yes, I have an early appointment in the morning. Besides, I'm sure you have early rounds to make and need a good night's sleep yourself," Elizabeth went on, not giving Sonny a chance to speak. "So I'll drive over to your place and arrive by six, then try to be home by nine."

Now Sonny realized what Lissa was doing, and a faint smile of combined frustration and admiration touched his lips.

"Lissa, I'll come get you," he said, using a gently firm tone.

Lissa's tone was every bit as firm as his, however.

"No, Sonny . . . I want to drive."

Sonny stifled a sigh, but after a short hesitation, decided to allow Lissa her small victory. After all, he intended to win the war.

"Fine," he agreed calmly.

"Good. Then I'll see you—"

"Lissa, there's just one thing I want to warn you about," Sonny interrupted.

"Oh?" Elizabeth had no idea what he was going to say, but she automatically felt wary.

"It's Maggie," Sonny said. "She's gotten a little possessive of me since I started to date, and she's not always gracious when she senses competition. I haven't come down as hard as I should have on her because I know how much she misses her mother . . ." Sonny hesitated about finishing the explanation with the words in his mind, then gave a mental shrug, and decided there was no point in hiding his intentions from Lissa. ". . . and because I haven't been serious enough about anyone to make a big thing of it . . . until now."

Elizabeth caught her breath in alarm, then relaxed. This was just one more reason for staying clear of Sonny Strotherton, and she was aware that no matter how determined she was to follow through on her intention to do just that, another good reason to bolster her willpower was welcome.

"I understand how she feels, Sonny," she said lightly, "and I won't take offense at anything she says or does. In fact," she added in a pointed way, "I'll make it as clear as I can to your daughter that, as far as I'm concerned, she has nothing to worry about."

Sonny gave a silent sigh of frustration at this indication that, despite what had happened between them the night before and what he'd said to her afterward, Lissa was still clinging to her intention to keep her distance from him. He saw no point in getting into an argument with her on the phone about it, however, so he merely said, somewhat dryly, "That wasn't what I had in mind, but thanks anyway, Lissa."

"You're welcome." Elizabeth chose to put her own interpretation on his words. "See you later, Sonny." And she hung up, glumly satisfied that she had set the stage for making her intentions even clearer to Sonny before the night was over.

Refusing to allow herself to think about Sonny for the rest of the afternoon, Elizabeth concentrated on re-memorizing the different bones of the human body instead, until it came time to get ready for her dinner date. Then, she washed her hair, dried and styled it, applied her makeup carefully, and put on a simple violet jersey dress with classic lines that matched her eyes. She wore pearl studs in her ears.

Well, I look like a woman who's in charge of her own destiny, she thought with wry humor as she inspected herself in her full-length mirror. *Now I just have to live up to my exterior.*

She controlled her nervousness on the drive to Sonny's home by mentally reciting different parts of the human anatomy to herself, and considered it fortunate that she hadn't reached the reproductive organs by the time she pulled into the Strotherton driveway. Then she concentrated on inspecting the Cape Cod design of the house.

"Traditional . . . of course," she murmured as she climbed out of the car. "Just like its owner."

Its owner opened the front door and came out to greet her just then, and she tried to be strictly objective as she swept her eyes over his handsome face, impressive physique, and the casual elegance of his navy blue, V-necked cashmere sweater with a white, open-necked shirt under it, and gray wool slacks.

By the time she completed her inspection, she wasn't feeling as objective as she wanted, but she maintained her poise as she walked toward Sonny with a pleasant smile on her lips.

"Good evening, Sonny," she said lightly as they met midway between the car and the house.

"Hello, Lissa," he answered in a voice Lissa was positive he didn't use on his regular dinner guests. "You look beautiful . . . as always."

She made herself glance away from the light of intimate welcome in his eyes. "I assure you, I don't always look like this," she said, and quickly changed the subject. "You have a lovely home, Sonny."

He took her arm to escort her to the house, but his eyes never left her face and his smile was as intimate as the look in his eyes.

"Thank you, Lissa. I'm glad you like it."

Inside the front hall, he took her coat and hung it in the closet while Elizabeth looked around and mentally complimented his former wife. There was nothing pretentious about the interior decorating. It was obvious that the former Mrs. Strotherton had had her family's comfort in mind more than creating a showplace, and Lissa approved.

After hanging up her coat and shutting the closet door, Sonny came close and put his arm around Elizabeth's waist, jerking her immediately back into an awareness of how attractive he was. She smelled the faint, pleasant scent of his aftershave, felt the warmth of his body and looked up into his warm gaze, and for just a moment, she wished with all her heart that there was nothing to stand between them . . . that this was the beginning of something wonderful for both of them instead of the last time they would ever be together.

"Come on," he said, his voice a deep caress. "I'll introduce you to Maggie."

As he guided her past the living room toward the back of the house, Elizabeth fought down her regrets and mentally reviewed all the reasons why she and Sonny shouldn't continue to see one another. And by the time they entered a large, pleasant family room where Maggie was watching television, she was back to being positive she was doing the right thing.

"Maggie, turn off the television and come meet Lissa," Sonny said with light firmness.

Maggie, clad in blue jeans and a light-blue sweater, reluctantly turned her blond head toward them, then back to the television for an instant, before she got to her feet to switch off the set. Then she dutifully presented herself in front of Sonny and Lissa for the introduction.

Elizabeth hid a smile at the subtle skill of Maggie's performance. She did nothing overtly rude her father could object to, but it was obvious she was merely being polite rather than eager to greet their guest.

"Hello," she said without any enthusiasm.

"Hello, Maggie," Lissa said matter-of-factly, and though she smiled, there was nothing in her manner that could be remotely construed as gushing or anxious to make a good impression on Sonny's daughter.

Maggie's eyes, so like her father's, showed a brief flash of puzzlement over Lissa's manner, then became blankly polite again.

"Sit down, Lissa," Sonny said, glancing between them warily. "Would you like a drink before dinner?"

"Thank you," Lissa sat down on the comfortable sofa in front of the fireplace. "I'll have a glass of wine if it isn't any trouble."

"No trouble at all." Sonny unconsciously smiled at Lissa in a way that revealed his feelings, failing to remember that Maggie was watching him like a hawk. "White or red?"

"White."

Sonny moved to the wet bar while Maggie seated herself in an easy chair that gave her a good view of Elizabeth.

"Daddy says you're going to medical school."

Maggie spoke too politely for Elizabeth to believe the child was genuinely interested in her plans, but she nodded. "Yes, I am. The spring semester starts next week, and I'll be very glad to get started finally."

"Why?" Maggie asked with just a hint of an edge in her voice.

"Because I've wanted to be a doctor like my father ever since I was a little girl," Elizabeth said simply, "but circumstances made it impossible for me to begin medical school until now. I'm glad the waiting's over."

"Lissa's father was a pediatrician, Maggie," Sonny said as he walked over from the bar with a glass of white wine in one hand and a glass of lemonade in the other. He handed the wine to Elizabeth, holding her gaze with his own for an instant as he did so—just long enough to make Elizabeth very aware of him as a man—then moved to where Maggie was sitting and handed her the lemonade.

"Like Dr. Cabot?" Maggie asked, glancing at Elizabeth with a curious combination of muted hostility and callous dismissal.

To her surprise, Elizabeth began to find Maggie's attitude slightly hurtful, but she clamped down on her unexpected reaction.

"Yes," she nodded. "As a matter of fact, Dr. Cabot is my godfather and he was also my pediatrician while I was growing up. I understand he's your doctor as well?"

Maggie looked surprised, then resentful. "I guess Daddy's told you all about me," she said, the edge to her voice very apparent now.

Sonny had returned from the wet bar, and he was just seating himself beside Lissa on the sofa. At hearing the tone of Maggie's voice, he lifted his head and gave her a sharp, meaningful look.

Elizabeth looked directly at Maggie and said, "No, as a matter of fact, he hasn't, Maggie. We haven't known one another long enough to do much talking at all."

Maggie frowned and opened her mouth to say something, but Sonny, afraid of what she might say, cut in.

"But I expect we'll be seeing a lot of Lissa from now on, Maggie," he said, giving his daughter a level, warning look, "and since you're such an important part of my life, I imagine we'll be talking about you from time to time. There's no reason to let it bother you, though, all right?"

It wasn't really a question, but Maggie's look clearly displayed what her answer would have been.

Though Elizabeth privately agreed that Sonny shouldn't allow his daughter to dictate his social life, she felt sorry for the girl; and since there was no reason for Maggie to be jealous of her, Elizabeth made an effort to ease the present unnecessary friction between father and daughter.

"Oh, I'm going to be so busy with school, I doubt I'll have time for much conversation with anyone about anything, other than other medical students about our classes," she said, projecting light humor into her voice and refusing to meet Sonny's eyes. Then she quickly turned the conversation in another direction. "Have you decided what kind of career interests you, Maggie?" she asked the girl before raising her glass of wine to her lips.

Maggie looked bored by the question, but she answered. "Well, if I could be anything I want, I'd like to be a rock singer like the Vixen," she said with a shrug.

Elizabeth choked on her wine, and it took a moment before she got her breath back.

"Are you all right?" Sonny asked anxiously.

"Yes . . . I'm fine," Elizabeth choked out. "I just swallowed some wine the wrong way."

At that moment, Mrs. Mullins appeared in the door to announce dinner, and Elizabeth had never been so glad of an interruption in her life. She felt like a fool for letting Maggie's announcement disturb her so much. After all, she'd known before tonight that Maggie was an all-out fan of the Vixen's, so why the shock?

"Great," she said hastily as she got to her feet. "I'm starved."

"Good," Sonny said as he got to his feet and stood beside her. "But are you sure you're all right?"

"She said she's fine, Daddy," Maggie said, impatient with his display of sympathy for their guest. "Come on, let's eat." And she led the way into the dining room.

The table could seat twelve, and Elizabeth felt a little ridiculous with only the three of them clustered at one end. Had the relationship with Sonny been going to continue, she would have suggested they eat in the breakfast nook, but since she never expected to dine in the Strotherton home again, she kept silent.

When Mrs. Mullins brought in green salads, Elizabeth smiled at her, liking the kind expression in the woman's brown eyes.

"Lissa, this is our housekeeper, Mrs. Mullins," Sonny introduced them. "Mrs. Mullins . . . Lissa Farrell."

"I'm very happy to meet you, Ms. Farrell," Mrs. Mullins said warmly.

"And it's a pleasure to meet you, Mrs. Mullins," Elizabeth replied.

Maggie was scowling until she caught Sonny's eye, and then she cleared her expression into a blank look of boredom.

All through the dinner, which was chicken breasts cooked in wine, parsleyed potatoes and green peas, followed by chocolate mousse, Maggie refused to initiate any conversation and answered only in monosyllables when asked a question.

Elizabeth soon ceased asking the girl questions, but Sonny, falling more and more out of patience with his daughter, insisted on forcing her to join in whenever possible.

Elizabeth breathed an inward sigh of relief when the meal was over. In another hour or so, she would be able to go home and try to forget that she was feeling just as attracted to Sonny as ever, despite her plan not to see him anymore. Maggie would obviously be pleased if Elizabeth Farrell dropped off the face of the earth rather than appear in their home again.

"How about a game of Chinese checkers?" Sonny said to Elizabeth when they were back in the family room.

She brightened immediately, much preferring to play a game than to have to talk until she and Sonny could speak privately.

"I'd love it," she said enthusiastically. "Dibs on the white marbles."

Maggie immediately gave her a hostile look. "My mom always played with the white ones," she said in a repressive tone.

For a moment, Sonny grimly regretted never spanking his daughter, thinking he might have gotten better results with her if he'd used the palm of his hand on her pert little bottom occasionally. But at the same time, he understood that she would probably have resented *anyone* using the marbles Caroline had always preferred, and in this case, her resentment was heightened because it was another woman who'd chosen them.

Elizabeth immediately understood and shrugged. "Then I'll take whatever color's left after you two choose," she said easily, and with a mischievous grin, added, "It doesn't really matter because I plan to beat the socks off both of you no matter what color you leave me."

"Oh, ho!" he scoffed. "Haven't you ever heard that pride goeth before a fall?"

Elizabeth's eyes sparkled at him. "Yes, I've heard that, but I didn't think you had," she said pointedly.

"But there's a difference in false pride and utter certainty," he said with a bland lack of modesty.

"Exactly," Elizabeth retorted. "And that's my position where Chinese checkers are concerned . . . utter confidence."

The game was hotly contested, and as Elizabeth moved her black marbles with skillful relentlessness toward the opposite triangle, she was positive that there were times when Maggie got so caught up in the play that she forgot she hadn't intended to enjoy herself.

Finally, Elizabeth jumped three of Sonny's blue marbles and one of Maggie's green ones and placed the last black marble in its slot.

Loudly applauding herself, she glanced between her two opponents, one of whom was looking at the board with disgust, and the other of whom was giving her a mock glare. "I win! I win!" she crowed with unselfconscious smugness. "Now what was that about pride going before a fall, Dr. Strotherton?"

"You aren't going to pretend you won because you deserved to, are you?" he scoffed. "That was sheer dumb luck!"

"Ha! Luck, my eye!" Elizabeth scoffed right back at him. "You're just a poor loser like most men! Right, Maggie?" she turned her laughing gaze in the girl's direction, looking for help.

But Maggie was back in character now, and she merely shrugged. "Daddy usually wins," she said dismissively as she got up from her chair. "May I be excused now, Daddy?" she asked, turning an innocent gaze on Sonny, who was giving her an impatient look. "I have a couple of chapters left to read for my book report."

Sonny hesitated, then shrugged. "Sure, honey," he said with muted disapproval in his voice. "Come give me a kiss."

Maggie obediently came around the game table and pecked her father on the cheek. Then she straightened and turned on a blankly polite expression for Elizabeth's benefit.

"Good night, Ms. Farrell," she said primly.

"Good night, Maggie," Elizabeth echoed, barely able to keep a straight face. "I enjoyed meeting you." And she had, in a rather peculiar way. At least, it was enlightening to see what the girl was capable of putting her father through whenever she sensed a rival for his affections.

When Maggie had disappeared from the room, Sonny turned to Lissa, and his gaze softened.

"Thanks for being such a good sport about Maggie's behavior," he said quietly. "I'm sorry she can be such a pill, but . . ."

"But she loved her mother," Elizabeth gently interrupted, "and she doesn't want anyone taking her place. Nor does she want to share the only parent she has left with anyone else. There's no need to apologize for her, Sonny. I would probably have felt the way she does if my father had dated after Mother died. I'm not even sure why he didn't." She shrugged, her gaze thoughtful. "Maybe he was waiting for me to be out on my own . . . but then it got to be too late."

Sonny reached over and covered Elizabeth's hand with his own.

"You still miss him, don't you?" he asked softly.

118

Drawn by the gentle sympathy she heard in his voice, Elizabeth made the mistake of looking into his eyes, and found herself caught by the warmth of his gaze.

"Yes . . . I still miss him," she said unsteadily and forced herself to look away. It was time she stopped enjoying Sonny's company so much and said what she had to.

"Sonny, there's something I have to tell you . . . ," she started to say, but Sonny gently raised her hand to his mouth at that moment and placed a warm kiss in her palm, making a frisson of pleasure spread immediately throughout her body.

"Sonny, don't—" she said weakly and tried to draw her hand away.

But Sonny sensed what she wanted to say and wanted to head her off. He had also felt her reaction to his kiss, and that was more than enough to keep him from letting her go. Instead, he moved his lips to her wrist, placing them with unerring accuracy over the pulse point there.

Elizabeth knew he felt the leap in her pulse and she curled her fingers together and tried again to pull free of him.

"Sonny, just because . . . well, it doesn't mean very much that . . . that there's a certain physical awareness between us," she said, but Sonny lifted his head at that instant and caught her gaze. Elizabeth swallowed when she saw the heat of arousal flickering in the blue of his eyes.

"Doesn't it?" he asked so softly she barely heard him.

She refused to answer, and she couldn't look away, and before she knew what he intended, Sonny was on his feet and had drawn her up into his arms.

He gave her no time to protest before his mouth took hers with hungry roughness, while his arms imprisoned her tightly against him. And as had happened each time he kissed her, Elizabeth found herself getting caught up in a now predictable response to his lovemaking.

She tried to stop it. Breaking away from his devouring mouth, she gasped, "Sonny, no . . . please . . . I need to talk to you, not—"

But Sonny was in no mood for talk, and his mouth covered hers again before she got any further with her protest. After two years of self-denial, he wanted nothing other than to plunder Lissa's soft mouth with his own and to feel her warm body melt against his. A dam was breaking inside him, and it was beyond Sonny to exercise the sort of self-control Lissa wanted from him . . . if that was what she really wanted, judging from the way she was beginning to respond to him.

Sonny was communicating his overpowering need for her to an extent that Lissa's senses, already vulnerable because of her very real attraction to him, were literally catching fire from his. No man had ever kissed her this hungrily or molded her against his body in such a way that Lissa felt as if they were becoming one entity.

Her mouth and body began to ache with a need to touch and explore his heated skin and the secrets of his maleness without the barrier of their clothing, and to have him touch her in the same way. She wanted to feel the pressure of his body over her . . . to experience a complete joining with this man whose throbbing need for her was so explosive it could awaken urgent needs of her own.

Sonny drew back slightly and gazed into her passion-clouded eyes, his own blazing with blue fire. "God, Lissa . . . ," he grated thickly between brief, biting kisses, "I'm on fire . . . I have to . . ."

At that instant, a young voice interrupted him. "Daddy, I—"

Maggie stopped short as she appeared in the doorway and saw the two of them locked in one another's arms.

Sonny immediately turned to look at his daughter, but Elizabeth, dazed herself, could tell that he was momentarily disoriented. And when she turned and saw the look of shocked hurt on Maggie's young face, she felt the same, as well as the beginnings of a deep sense of shame.

"Oh, Daddy, how could you!" Maggie choked out, and with tears brimming in her eyes, she whirled away to run toward the stairs.

Sonny stared after his daughter for a long moment, then turned back to Elizabeth with such confusion in his face that Elizabeth could tell he was torn between frustration and guilt.

Elizabeth quickly stepped out of his arms. "Go to her, Sonny," she said shakenly.

Sonny shut his eyes and raked a trembling hand through his hair. Then he shook his head and looked at her with torment in his eyes.

"Lissa, I don't want to hurt her, but she's got to understand—" he started to say.

Elizabeth shook her head. "But she needs time, Sonny," she said, and took a deep breath to try to quell the shaking inside her.

"Just go to her, Sonny," she repeated. "You're all she's got, and she needs to be reassured that you aren't going to abandon her. It's hard to be rational about something like that at her age."

Or any age, she added silently as a sudden longing for her own father welled up inside her. If he were here to advise her . . . or just to listen to her . . . But there was no sense wishing for the impossible, so she merely stepped forward and gave Sonny a gentle push in the direction Maggie had taken.

"All right, Lissa," Sonny finally agreed in a gruff way that told her he was feeling very frustrated. "Wait for me. I'll be down after I've talked to Maggie."

Instead of agreeing, Elizabeth simply repeated, "Go on, Sonny. She needs you."

Before he left her, however, Sonny raised his hand and placed it against Elizabeth's flushed cheek, telling her with his eyes how much he regretted the interruption in what had been happening between them.

Elizabeth felt an almost overwhelming desire to cling to him and keep him with her, but she forced herself to keep her hands at her side.

Then she watched as he walked away to go to Maggie. And the moment she heard a door close upstairs, she went to the closet in the front hall, got her coat, and quietly let herself out of the house. She knew if she stayed and waited for him, he would hold her forever.

CHAPTER TEN

Elizabeth had finally fallen into a restless sleep when the sound of the doorbell startled her awake again. Confused, she glanced at the clock radio on her bedside table, and when she saw that it was eleven o'clock, she frowned. Who could be at her door at this hour?

Elizabeth was alone in the house and she was not the type to get nervous about it usually, but then usually no one rang her doorbell this late.

Throwing the covers back, she got up and slipped her arms in the sleeves of a terry-cloth robe and as she walked toward her bedroom door, it finally dawned on her who it might be, and she hesitated with her hand on the doorknob. The last thing she needed right then was a conversation with Sonny . . . especially when she doubted conversation was all he had in mind.

The sound of the doorbell echoed through the house twice more in rapid succession, and Elizabeth, who had been thinking about ignoring the summons, found she couldn't do it and jerked the bedroom door open.

She made her way downstairs, during which time the doorbell rang again, and when she'd crossed the living room, she turned on the porch light, then peeked through the hole in the door and found that, just as she'd feared, it was Sonny standing there.

Reluctantly, she unlocked the inner door, opened it, and stood facing him through the glass of the storm door.

"I know it's late, Lissa," Sonny said as she stood frowning at him. "But it's important. I need to talk to you."

Elizabeth very much doubted if talking was all he had in mind, and she didn't feel up to the struggle of fighting herself as well as him, but there didn't seem anything else to do but let him in, so she silently opened the storm door and Sonny stepped across the threshold.

"Thanks, Lissa," he said when the door was closed behind him and they stood facing one another, Sonny in his topcoat and Lissa in her robe. "But I wouldn't be here if you'd waited for me earlier," he added in a tone of gentle remonstrance.

Elizabeth sighed tiredly. "I didn't see the point, Sonny," she said simply. Then she nodded at his coat. "Take your coat off, and I'll fix us some hot chocolate."

"That isn't necessary," Sonny said as he slipped out of his coat.

Elizabeth didn't answer. She merely took his coat, hung it up in the hall closet, then led the way to the kitchen.

Sonny didn't sit down as Elizabeth got milk out of the refrigerator, poured it in a pan and set it on the stove to heat, then got a can of chocolate mix and two mugs out of the cabinet. He stood near her, his eyes taking a warmly affectionate inventory of her tousled hair, clean face and sleepy eyes, short white terry-cloth robe and fluffy pink slippers.

When Elizabeth glanced at him inquiringly, he smiled.

"I thought you said you didn't always look beautiful." His voice was soft and deep, and thoroughly alarming to Elizabeth in her groggy state.

"Shouldn't you be asleep?" she asked, refusing to deal with his compliment. "My dad never got enough sleep."

Sonny's gaze was purposeful. "Some things are more important than sleep, Lissa," he said quietly, "and believe me, I couldn't have slept tonight before talking to you even if I'd felt inclined to try."

Elizabeth quickly looked away and started fumbling in a drawer for a couple of spoons.

"How's Maggie?" she tried to delay what she was positive was coming.

Sonny's expression sobered. "I think she cried herself to sleep after we had our little talk."

Elizabeth glanced at him again before moving to the stove to see if the milk was hot yet.

"Sonny, I don't want to cause Maggie pain," she said, staring down at the milk in the pan. "Especially when there's no reason for it."

Sonny ignored the last sentence. "I don't want to cause Maggie pain either," he said quietly, "but I don't see any way around it. It doesn't really have anything to do with you specifically. Maggie would try to sabotage any relationship I had with a woman. And since I have no intention of remaining single for the rest of my life, I can't let her think she's going to be able to prevent me from marrying again."

Elizabeth privately agreed with Sonny's position, but she hadn't liked one little bit being the cause of the look she'd seen on Maggie's young face that evening.

The milk started simmering, so Elizabeth turned off the stove, spooned some chocolate mix into the mugs, then poured the milk over it and stirred it. "Here, Sonny," she said as she handed him his mug and led the way to the table in the breakfast nook.

When they were seated across from one another, Sonny made no effort to drink his hot chocolate, while Elizabeth sipped hers more out of nervousness than thirst.

The silence between them grew, and every time Elizabeth gave Sonny a quick glance, the look on his face increased her nervousness. Finally, she couldn't stand it anymore.

"Sonny, you know why I left earlier instead of waiting for you," she said hurriedly. "Please . . . let it go. Don't . . . don't keep asking me for something I can't give you."

"I wouldn't if I really thought you couldn't," he replied calmly. "But you keep giving me double messages, Lissa. Which do you want me to believe? Your words or the way you respond when I touch you?"

Lissa closed her eyes and gave a weary sigh. Sonny had a point. Opening her eyes, she gazed at him beseechingly.

"Sonny, I admit it . . . when you kiss me and hold me, I go a little crazy. But there are reasons . . ." She caught herself, bit her lip and looked away, unaware that to Sonny, she looked as though she were hiding a guilty secret.

Frowning, he leaned forward and put his hand over hers. The contact made Elizabeth jerk and she quickly turned to face him again.

"I'd like to hear those reasons, Lissa," he said quietly. "I'd like to know what's more important than what happens between us when we touch."

Elizabeth opened her mouth to repeat the weak excuse that she wanted to concentrate exclusively on her medical studies, but something in Sonny's face told her such an effort would be useless. Which left what? She couldn't lie and say she had no interest in him whatsoever because he knew better.

"I . . . don't think we're compatible other than physically, Sonny," she said, groping for something he might believe.

"How can you possibly know that, Lissa?" Sonny responded with muted impatience. "That's not a reason, that's a copout! We haven't had time to learn enough about one another for you to come to such a conclusion. In fact, if I wanted to jump to a conclusion of my own at this early stage of our relationship, I'd say just the opposite . . . that our mutual love of medicine and the way we react to one another physically gives us a very real basis for thinking we'll be compatible in other ways."

He paused, then gave her a searching look. "But are you thinking that two physicians in the same family is one too much? Does that worry you?"

Elizabeth mutely shook her head, and Sonny shook his head in frustrated puzzlement.

"Then what is it, Lissa? It isn't the demands of medical school, it isn't because you aren't attracted to me, and it isn't Maggie either. You've been resisting the pull between us almost from the moment we met, and I don't understand it when there's such a powerful magnetism between us . . . so powerful that we deserve a chance to see if there can be more!"

Elizabeth hated being backed into a corner, and she was growing angry with Sonny because if he weren't such a rigid, prejudiced stuffed shirt, neither of them would be in this position. They could have done exactly what Sonny was trying to persuade her to do . . . begun to see one another and perhaps had a chance for a wonderful relationship! Instead, because of the sort of man he was, she couldn't trust him enough to tell him the truth. She was almost positive the truth was the last thing he wanted to hear!

Jerking her hand from beneath his, she clenched it into a fist and lashed out at him.

"I can't explain, Sonny! Now stop badgering me!"

The outburst sounded so desperate and Lissa's manner was so strange that Sonny was taken completely by surprise. Then he frowned as a possible explanation for her behavior hit him.

"Lissa . . . ," he said slowly, dread in his voice, "is there someone else? Is that why . . . ?"

"No!" she burst out, much too quickly to sound convincing. Then she made things worse, from Sonny's point of view, by adding indignantly, "And anyway, my private life is no concern of yours!"

Of course, Elizabeth meant something entirely different from the way Sonny took her words, and he sat back and just looked at her in silence while he tried to absorb the blow she'd just dealt him.

Elizabeth could tell from the expression on his face how much she'd hurt him, and she was torn between a strong desire to ease his hurt and an equally strong desire to remain quiet and let him think whatever he liked. Perhaps it would be better if Sonny thought there was another man in her life. Maybe then he'd leave her alone. But such a solution to her dilemma left a bad taste in her mouth. She was becoming thoroughly sick of secrets and lies and having to behave contrary to her basic nature.

While she wavered, unable to look Sonny in the eye, Sonny digested the fact that he might very well have a rival and, for whatever reason, Lissa wanted to keep his identity a secret, and he tried to deal with the torrent of jealousy suffusing him.

He wondered why the possibility that she had another man in her life hadn't occurred to him before. After all, a beautiful woman like Lissa must collect admirers by the dozens. But of course, she hadn't said so before and she wasn't saying so now. In fact, she'd pretended she didn't want a serious relationship with anyone for the present. Why?

A possibility occurred to Sonny that he didn't want to deal with.

Nor could he really accept it. Lissa just wasn't the type of woman to become involved with a married man, even if that might explain why she was behaving so secretively.

That led to another possibility, however, that gave Sonny some hope. If she was involved with someone else, that didn't mean she was irrevocably committed to him yet, did it? If she was, wouldn't she say so? And if she wasn't, he still had a chance with her. Even if she thought she was committed to someone else, Sonny couldn't accept that she could respond to him the way she did if that other commitment was valid.

As he looked at her and saw the trapped expression in her eyes, Sonny cursed himself for the way he'd been pressuring her. If he was going to win her, it wouldn't be by making her so unhappy. It was time to lighten up and make her glad to be with him instead of dreading his presence.

A trace of a smile began to tug at his mouth as he reached over and took her hand in his again. She looked at him with a startled expression, and when she saw his smile, her eyes widened in puzzlement.

"Lissa, perhaps because I've already got my life pretty much in order, I've been forgetting that you aren't in the same position and I've been pressuring you too hard and too soon to do things my way. That isn't fair. I realize that now. Would you consider continuing to see me if I were more patient and less intense about our relationship?"

Elizabeth stared at him, impressed by his apparent sincerity and his willingness to try to see things from her point of view. A tiny flicker of hope that he might not be as rigid as she'd presumed he was began to glow inside her, fanned by the stark truth that, despite all the objective reasons she had for thinking it would be best to steer clear of Sonny, she didn't really want to. He was right about the powerful magnetism between them.

Sensing that Lissa was wavering, Sonny concealed his inner relief and growing optimism about her feelings for him and calmly went on.

"I won't deny that I'd skip this stage in our relationship if it was up to me, but you know that anyway. And if you'll feel more comfortable taking things more slowly, I understand. I'd just like for us to have a chance to really come to know one another and see what happens, Lissa. Wouldn't you?"

Without answering, though she really wanted the same thing, Elizabeth leaned her head on her free hand, closed her eyes, and tried to resolve the conflict between her head and her heart. This new side of Sonny was so appealing, it made her doubt that she'd judged him fairly. And even if she'd been right about him, perhaps if he came to know her well enough as the person she was and cared enough about her, it wouldn't matter so much to him that she'd once been the Vixen and had deceived him.

Sonny squeezed her hand and Elizabeth opened her eyes to find him looking at her in a way that melted her heart. Suddenly, she doubted very much that a man who could look so warmly caring and who'd just given proof that he was willing to be patient and understanding with her would turn nasty at learning her small secret.

But there was still a tiny kernel of caution inside her that said, "Wait. Get to know him better before you trust him completely. Your career as a doctor is too important to risk the sort of obstacles Sonny could put in your path if he can't separate the Vixen from Lissa Farrell."

"I . . . suppose we could . . . see what happens," she found herself saying, and immediately she felt a tremendous upsurge of relief that she didn't have to send Sonny away and never see him again.

Sonny's expression echoed her relief to such an extent that Elizabeth had to smile, and then he was on his feet, laughingly pulling her up with him, and hugging her tightly in his arms. And it felt so good to be there, that Elizabeth was doubly glad she hadn't sent him away.

Sonny's mouth was drawn to Elizabeth's as inevitably as parched earth calls for rain, and she met his kiss so eagerly that he was positive she couldn't be in love with another man. However, the thought of her in another man's arms sparked exactly the sort of fervent, possessive desire in him that he'd promised himself he'd tone down in order to try to win her. But that was when she'd been sitting across the table from him, not kissing him as uninhibitedly as she was now, and Sonny temporarily forgot his good intentions.

His hands moved automatically to unfasten the belt of her robe, and then he slid his hands inside it to touch the warmth of her skin through her silk nightgown. As he did so, a lightning memory of holding the Vixen like this skittered through Sonny's mind, and for an instant, he was horrified at connecting a woman like that with Lissa.

But then, Lissa stirred erotically under the movement of his hands and Sonny's physical reaction was intense . . . as intense as it had been that night in the Vixen's dressing room. And it suddenly occurred to him that if he did win Lissa, he would have every man's dream . . . a woman who could stir him physically as intensely as the most erotic fantasy, but who would be real and would also have all the other qualities a man wanted in a wife—intelligence, character, and the capacity to love him unreservedly.

"Lissa . . . Lissa . . . ," he said, his voice raggedly reflecting his combined desire and wonder. "God, you're everything a man could want."

His words jolted Lissa slightly out of her preoccupation with her own senses, making her feel guiltily anxious. And even as his mouth smothered hers again, she was beginning to realize that keeping the truth from Sonny was going to present some difficulties she hadn't considered when agreeing to continue seeing him. Would Sonny still consider her "everything a man could want" when he learned she'd been lying to him and that she was the same woman he considered little better than a tramp?

And could she make love for the first time in her life with a man she considered it necessary to lie to . . . a man who might very well reject her when he did learn the truth?

Unaware of the turmoil in Lissa's mind, Sonny concentrated on filling senses too long deprived and evoking the wholehearted response he needed and wanted from the woman he already knew was everything he'd been seeking since losing his wife.

His hands sought the warm secrets of her body, performed the intimacies he couldn't bear thinking of another man sharing with her, while his lips and tongue devoured the sweetness of her mouth.

Lissa shuddered as one of Sonny's hands covered her breast, while the other slipped to her bottom and cupped her against the heat in his loins, while his tongue plunged and explored the interior of her mouth and made her dizzy with desire. Her mind momentarily lost touch with reality as she became lost in rolling waves of ever-heightening sensual response to Sonny's enveloping assault.

Sonny was lost to reality as well as Lissa clung to him and permitted him free access to the whole silken, heated temptation of her lovely body. He didn't care if he ever surfaced from this intense waking fantasy.

But suddenly it wasn't enough to touch her through her gown and to stand with her melting against him when he wanted her naked beneath him, submissive and aching in the way he ached for the ultimate melding of his body with hers.

"Lissa, come upstairs," he grated against her mouth. "Let me love you totally . . . don't make me wait any longer . . ."

As his hands came up to brush her robe from her shoulders, Lissa opened her eyes, and through the drugged haze her aroused senses permitted, saw the desperate urgency in Sonny's, just as she'd heard it in his voice. She wanted desperately to give him what he wanted. Yet, a small, thin thread of concern struggled for life in her mind. If she did go to bed with Sonny, she didn't want them to have any secrets between them . . . she wanted Sonny to make love to her knowing he was making love to the Vixen as well as Elizabeth Farrell.

Then Sonny caught her mouth in a kiss that was so demanding, she feared it might be too late to stop him, which finally gave her the impetus to try. Tearing her mouth from his, she dropped her head on his shoulder, panting for breath, while she brought her hands up to his chest in a restraining motion.

"Lissa . . ."

The ragged, masculinely demanding way Sonny said her name thrilled her, and she fought for the strength to resist him.

All she could manage for the moment was to shake her head, but when she did, Sonny quickly raised his hand to the back of her head, entwining his fingers in her thick hair and making her raise her head to look at him. His eyes were fairly blazing a denial of her intention, and she could only stare back at him with her ambivalence reflected in her eyes.

"God, Lissa, you can't mean it!" he grated with such frustration in his tone that Lissa flinched with the guilt she was feeling at allowing things to go so far and then trying to back off.

But Sonny didn't interpret her flinch correctly. He thought she was reacting to the pressure he was putting on her when he'd promised he wouldn't.

"Oh, God, Lissa, I didn't intend . . . but if you only knew how hard this is for me . . ."

Sonny stopped speaking because inside, he was raging with thwarted desire and frustration because he didn't know how to dispose of whatever obstacle was in the path of his own happiness, and, he was convinced, of Lissa's. But he'd made a promise, and if temporarily denying himself what he most wanted in the world was the only way he could win Lissa Farrell completely, he'd stick to it.

Sonny drew back slightly, and Elizabeth was so torn with conflicting desires herself, she couldn't find anything to say and stood miserably looking down at the floor, clutching her arms around herself against the sudden chill that had enveloped her at losing contact with Sonny.

He hesitated, then bent, picked up her robe from the floor and gently put it around her shoulders.

Lissa clutched it around her, and finally found the courage to meet Sonny's gaze, her own very vulnerable and filled with regret.

Sonny's smile was wryly self-mocking. "I guess I'm going to have to dredge up more willpower than I've just shown if I'm going to keep my promise to you," he said, his tone slightly grim.

Lissa responded with the simple truth. "Perhaps you're not the only one who needs more willpower, Sonny," she said quietly. "I'm not very proud of what I just did. It wasn't fair to you. I just . . . don't seem to be able to behave very rationally when I'm in your arms. I'm surprised I was able to stop when I did."

Her confession eased Sonny's torment considerably. And as he remembered how Lissa had responded to him, and how difficult it had been for her to stop, his self-confidence began to return, along with his optimism that he was eventually going to win Lissa Farrell for his own.

"I noticed you weren't indifferent to me," he said softly, and he began to smile at her in a warmly teasing way that eased the tension inside Lissa.

Slowly, she began to smile back at him, and the way he was taking what had happened made her own optimism about their relationship escalate.

"I guess I'd better go home before I do something foolish again," he said lightly, stepping back. "Come on, Lissa. Show me the door. Just don't kick me out for good, okay?"

"Okay," she said softly, her smile soft and encouraging.

When he had his coat on, he stepped close and cupped her face in his hands. He smiled when she lifted her mouth for the kiss she thought he wanted.

"No, I'm not going to kiss you again," he said huskily, "I don't dare right now. But it's nice to see I wouldn't be rejected if I could trust myself to stop at one kiss."

Lissa stared at him with wide, solemn eyes, and he bent and touched his lips to her forehead, then let her go and stuffed his hands in his pockets.

"I'll call you tomorrow, Lissa. I may have promised not to rush you, but that doesn't mean you won't find me on your doorstep every time you give me permission to be there."

Instantly, Elizabeth had a vision of Sonny running into Danny, Jay, and Darla, and her expression sobered.

When she saw that her reaction hurt Sonny, however, she quickly stepped forward and slipped her arms around his waist, leaning her head on his chest for a moment.

Sonny was relieved and withdrew his hands from his pockets to hold her, taking care not to hug her as tightly as he would have preferred.

Lissa returned the hug, then stepped back. "Yes, Sonny," she said firmly. "Call me tomorrow."

The tension inside Sonny abated immediately, and his smile caressed her for a brief instant before he opened the door, blew her a kiss, and stepped across the threshold.

Elizabeth stood for a moment watching him walk away, before she closed the door, leaned back against it, and with her eyes closed, wondered how long she could continue to see Sonny before he and the rest of her unusual household finally ran across one another and the truth exploded in her face.

I'll manage to keep them apart somehow, she thought, feeling slightly depressed that she had let herself in for another long bout of evasions and half-truths when she'd thought she was through with all that.

As she settled down in bed a few minutes later, she hoped the risk she was taking for Sonny Strotherton would be worth it. Otherwise, she might not only end up with a damaged reputation in Boston's medical community. She might also end up with a broken heart.

CHAPTER ELEVEN

Elizabeth slept restlessly for the rest of the night. She kept waking up wondering how to keep Sonny and Danny apart, and worrying about falling so much in love with Sonny that she might end up heartbroken should she come to trust him with the truth and he handled it badly.

At six o'clock the next morning, she was sitting up in bed with a scowl of tired frustration on her face. This was supposed to be the best time in her life—the time when she embarked on the training that would allow her to realize her lifelong goal of becoming a physician. But because of her brother's musical ambitions and her would-be lover's prejudices, she was caught in the middle of a dilemma which was making it very difficult for this to be the best time of her life!

"Damn men, anyway!" she muttered as she got up to start the day far earlier than she wanted to. "Why can't they all be like Dad was—tolerant and loving and giving, instead of selfish, single-minded spoiled brats?"

But an instant later, she was turning the criticism back on herself. "You sacrificed for Danny, but only up to a point," she thought ruefully. "You're as single-minded about becoming a doctor as Danny is about music and Sonny seems to be about pursuing you. And Sonny faces the same risk of getting hurt if he falls in love with you as you do in falling in love with him. Furthermore, if he does get hurt, it will be because of your lies."

Tell him the truth before it gets to be too late, Lissa, she told herself as she stepped into the shower. *Take the risk and do it!*

But it was easier to say the words than to act on them. By telling the truth she had to worry about Sonny's reaction and she also had to be concerned about the medical community finding out. She didn't want to be laughed out of the profession before she even got started!

Sonny was in an excellent mood. Even Maggie's sullen expression at breakfast couldn't dampen it. He did make an effort to get through to her, though.

"Come here, pet," he said when breakfast was over, and he pulled her into his lap and gave her a big hug. "Be happy for me, sweetheart," he coaxed when her expression didn't lighten. "I've been awfully lonely since we lost your mother."

"You've got me," Maggie said resentfully.

"And I love having you," Sonny agreed. "But one day you'll leave me and take up your own life, and—"

"So marry someone after I'm gone," Maggie interrupted, her expression stubbornly unrelenting.

Sonny sighed and shook his head. "I can't wait that long, Maggie," he said quietly. "Not now that I've found someone I think I can love."

Maggie's sullenness didn't relent, and without another word, she hopped off his lap and went to get ready for school.

Shaking his head, Sonny watched her go, then went to call Elizabeth.

"Have dinner with me tonight?" he asked when he had her on the line. "I'm on call, so we might be interrupted, but I want to see you."

"All right," Elizabeth answered softly. Hearing Sonny's voice was enough to make her forget momentarily the problems seeing him were causing her. "Why don't you come here?"

"I'd love to," Sonny agreed. "Is seven o'clock all right?"

"It's fine."

After clearing up the last few details which would allow her to start medical school the next Monday, Elizabeth spent the rest of the day studying again, both because she felt she needed to and because she wanted to keep her mind off other, more troubling things . . . such as whether to tell Sonny the truth that night.

That evening, however, when he took her in his arms and kissed her passionately before he even had his coat off, and she responded with her own hot passion, Lissa suddenly knew she wasn't going to tell him the truth yet. Sonny had already become too important to her to risk driving him away. Before she told him she had to be sure that he would be willing to overlook such a little thing as the fact that she'd once been the Vixen.

After two lovely evenings together Monday and Tuesday, during which Elizabeth found herself liking Sonny more and more, as well as being totally turned on by him, she was forced to make a flimsy excuse to avoid seeing him until Friday. Danny and the Foursome were due back the next day, but would leave again Friday morning.

"I'm sorry, Sonny," she said after telling him she couldn't see him for a few days. He was so obviously trying to conceal how disappointed he was for her sake that she was filled with guilt and self-disgust over her choice to continue to deceive him. But she was still afraid she would lose him if she told him the truth.

But if the thought of losing him is this bad now, she thought miserably, *what will it be like later?*

Sonny was about to leave to go home, and he was trying hard to conceal his hurt over his suspicions about Lissa and another man. When he thought he had himself in hand, he drew her into his arms.

"I'll miss you," he said softly, holding her close. "But if I have to, I guess I can make it until Friday night."

He kissed her then, and the jealousy that wracked him imparted a fervor to the kiss that sent shivers of delight through Elizabeth.

It was becoming increasingly hard for her to deny both of them the fulfillment of loving one another totally. But even if she was behaving badly according to her own standards in denying him the truth about her, she knew she couldn't commit the ultimate dishonesty of sharing the sort of intimacy with him that cried out for truth and honesty beforehand . . . and trust on her part as well as his.

Though she kissed him back, Sonny sensed that she was feeling ambivalent, and his frustration and heartache grew. Finally, he had to let her go before he tried to force her to give him the complete, wholehearted response he needed so badly.

"I'd better go," he said quietly. "It's getting late."

His manner tore at Elizabeth's heart, and impulsively, she cradled his face in her hands. "One day . . . ," she started to say, then stopped herself before she could say too much.

Sonny raised his brows inquiringly, but when Elizabeth looked away, he took a deep breath and accepted that his patience was going to have to stretch a little farther. At least, he seemed to be making some progress. She seemed to be coming to like him more and more.

Elizabeth felt both disconsolate at not being able to see Sonny for a few days, and yet hopeful that his apparent willingness to work for their relationship meant he would forgive her for not being honest with him.

"Sonny, I'll miss you, too," she said sincerely, giving him her sweetest smile. Then, she leaned forward and kissed him with slow thoroughness. When she straightened at last, the look of sweet, lambent sexuality in her eyes was enough to encourage Sonny to endure his frustration and take heart that his perseverance and patience would eventually win him his heart's desire.

"Good night, Lissa," he said, his voice husky and strained. "I'll see you Friday."

As Elizabeth watched him leave, she was aware that her feelings for him were escalating so quickly, she was one step away from being hopelessly in love with him.

Though Elizabeth wasn't surprised to find herself missing Sonny the next evening, she muffled it by giving free rein to her curiosity about how things had gone with the Foursome, and by the time Danny and Darla and Jay arrived home, just in time for dinner, she was about to burst.

She looked for signs as she hugged each of them in turn, and was much relieved when she saw that Danny didn't seem to be out of temper, and Darla didn't appear to be upset.

"Well," she demanded when their coats were put away and they sat down in the living room to relax for a few minutes before they ate. "How did it go?"

"It went all right," Danny admitted with only a trace of grudgingness in his voice. "No one knew the difference apparently."

Elizabeth was relieved, but she was also put out with Danny because he was being so grudging about the whole matter. She could tell from the look on Darla's face that she wasn't all that pleased with Danny either.

Jay, stretched out on the sofa, grinned to himself, but Elizabeth caught his look and put him on the spot.

"Jay, what do you think?" she asked pleasantly. "Did the audiences react to Darla all right?"

"She did fine as far as I'm concerned," he said. "What's for dinner?"

"Yankee pot roast," Elizabeth said, her tone relieved. But she turned away from Jay and addressed Darla next. "Did you feel comfortable, Darla?" she asked solicitously. "No jitters?"

Darla shrugged and winked at Elizabeth. "No jitters," she said calmly, "and I think I did better than all right. I got a standing ovation after singing Danny's new song, so I must have done something right."

"It's a good song," Danny put in, getting to his feet. "Let's eat."

Disgusted with Danny's refusal to give Darla any credit at all, Elizabeth scowled at him. But she knew her brother well enough that she didn't waste her breath taking him to task, which wouldn't have done the least good and would only have put him in a foul mood.

"All right, let's eat," she agreed, getting to her feet.

After dinner, Danny went upstairs to his room to work on a new song, and Jay left for a karate lesson. Elizabeth and Darla sat in the library chatting, and after Elizabeth had heard all about the concert, she noticed that Darla was looking at her in a curious way.

"Is something bothering you?" Darla asked.

Elizabeth hesitated, but she felt so comfortable with Darla, she finally decided to confide in her. It would be nice to talk to somebody about Sonny.

Slowly, guiltily she explained about Sonny, and when she was done, Darla was staring at her in amazement.

"Why would you want someone who's such a snob?" she asked bluntly. "Surely, you're not ashamed of Danny or your own musical talent either, for that matter. One doesn't create the kind of sensation you did unless there's solid talent behind all the makeup and costumes."

Elizabeth shook her head. "No, I'm not in the least ashamed of Danny, Darla. And though I don't want to make a career of music, I wouldn't be human if I didn't appreciate the kind of response I got as the Vixen, and I'm not ashamed of what I did. But you have to understand the medical community, Darla. Some of its members are very staid and traditional, and still accept women doctors grudgingly. They surely wouldn't believe how serious I am about medicine if they knew I'd been the Vixen."

"But from what you've said, Sonny admires you for wanting to become a doctor," Darla objected.

Elizabeth nodded. "You'd have to have been there to see how he reacted to the Vixen, though," she said gloomily.

Darla snorted. "He couldn't have reacted too badly if he came backstage and kissed you," she pointed out with dry sarcasm.

Elizabeth frowned, thinking about the way Sonny had behaved that night. "I still don't know why he did come backstage," she said thoughtfully. "And I kissed him, Darla . . . at least, I started the kiss."

"And he finished it." Darla nodded.

"Yes, he did . . . ," Elizabeth said slowly, "but he did it in such a curious way. It was like he didn't want to, but he couldn't help himself. But I guess that's not surprising after what I'd just told him," he grimaced. "He thought I was a tramp."

Darla looked annoyed.

Elizabeth smiled ruefully. "Darla, you have to admit that not many respectable men would react favorably to a woman who'd just told them she was going to sleep with a man to pay him for giving her a job!"

Darla shrugged. "I suppose not," she said grudgingly, "but you said he didn't like the Vixen from the beginning. Do you think it's because his daughter is so infatuated with the Foursome, and especially the Vixen?"

"I honestly don't know if that's all of it or only part of it." Elizabeth sighed. "I wish I did."

Darla gazed at her sympathetically. "Well, I'm not much good at handing out advice," she said gently, "but I think the smartest thing for you to do is to find out. You're going to have to tell him someday, Lissa. Don't you think you'd better do it before the two of you get in over your heads? Both of you can get badly hurt if you wait too long."

Elizabeth knew Darla's advice was sound, but she was afraid to take it just yet.

"Well, I'm pretty tired," Darla said lightly as she reached over and patted Elizabeth's hand. "So if you don't mind, I think I'll go upstairs and go to bed."

Elizabeth nodded absently, and it was only when Darla had reached the door that she remembered to ask about her friend's mother.

"Darla, did your mother go to that physician I recommended?" she asked.

Darla turned, her expression serious. "Yes, she did," she said gravely. "And he recommended she have the operation. But Mom's still dithering about making a decision."

Elizabeth was surprised, but she didn't show it. "Well, it isn't a life-threatening matter," she said soothingly, "so it won't hurt her to think about it for a while. Just give her some time."

Darla nodded, said good night, and went upstairs to bed.

Elizabeth sat on, wrestling with her own problems. She knew what she needed to do. It was only a question of when to do it.

CHAPTER TWELVE

After the Foursome left Friday, Elizabeth was looking forward to her evening with Sonny, and she was extremely disappointed when he called and canceled.

"Maggie's coming down with something. She has a temperature of 102 degrees right now, so I think I'd better stick around and keep an eye on her until I know what she's got."

"Yes, I think you should," Elizabeth agreed, trying not to sound as disappointed as she felt.

"I've missed you," Sonny then said, and Elizabeth's heart lightened.

"I've missed you, too, Sonny," she said with warm sincerity.

Sonny was so pleased by her words and tone that it was almost enough to make up for the jealousy he'd been experiencing over the past three days thinking of her with someone else. It was also enough to make him regret more heartily than ever that he couldn't see her that evening.

"Lissa," he said, "if it turns out nothing serious is wrong with Maggie, can I see you tomorrow?"

Elizabeth readily agreed, and then she had a sudden thought. If things between her and Sonny worked out, there was still the problem of Maggie's jealousy of her to be dealt with, and she knew that taking Sonny away from his daughter when she was ill wasn't going to win her any points with Maggie.

"Sonny," she said, "why don't we spend tomorrow with Maggie? She could probably use the company if she can't go anywhere with her friends."

Sonny was torn between his desire to be alone with Lissa and his admiration for her consideration for his daughter's feelings.

"That's kind of you, Lissa," he said softly. "Are you sure you don't mind?"

Of course, she would rather have been alone with Sonny, but Elizabeth merely said, "I don't mind, Sonny."

"Then I'll call you in the morning and tell you how she's doing," Sonny said, and they rang off.

Elizabeth had had enough of studying for a while, and rather than spend the evening alone missing Sonny, she called Aunt Sarah and invited her and Uncle Ferris over for dinner.

It turned out that Maggie merely had a cold, so at Sonny's invitation, Elizabeth drove over there the next morning and the three of them played games and watched television.

To Elizabeth's relief, Maggie showed no overt hostility toward her. The girl was rather quiet, but Elizabeth attributed that to the fact that Maggie wasn't feeling well, and began to feel optimistic that things were going to work out all right.

Sonny felt so much the same that by late afternoon, he thought it would be all right to suggest that he and Lissa go out for dinner together and let Maggie have an early night.

Elizabeth happily accepted the invitation, and when Sonny left her and Maggie alone for a moment to take a call, she was totally unprepared for the attack Maggie immediately launched.

With a hostile gleam in her blue eyes, Maggie said scornfully, "You think you've got it made, don't you?"

"What?" Maggie was astonished by the change in Maggie. Before Sonny had left the room, the girl had been smiling. She wasn't smiling now.

"Don't play dumb," Maggie snapped. "I can tell by the way you look at Daddy that you think you're in love with him. But I don't believe you are. I think you just want to marry a good-looking doctor who has a nice house and a lot of money!"

Elizabeth stared at Maggie as anger welled inside her. She took a moment to control her temper, and then decided Maggie Strotherton needed a good lesson in being able to take it as well as dish it out.

"I have some news for you, Maggie," she said firmly, projecting quiet confidence into her tone. "I can probably buy and sell your father if I want to, my house is as nice as this one if not nicer, and since my father was a doctor, and I'm going to be one myself, I don't feel the need to marry into the medical community to enhance my social status. In fact, if your Dad and I should get married, it will be because we love one another and for no other reason."

She got to her feet, holding the girl's gaze as Maggie stared up at her looking belligerent . . . and worried.

"I'll tell you something else, Maggie," Elizabeth went on quietly. "I think you have the potential to become a fine person. But if you don't learn to stop thinking only of yourself . . . if you don't learn that loving isn't just a one-way street, all taking and no giving . . . you'll never amount to anything. I think your father deserves more kindness from you than you're showing him by trying to get rid of every woman who might give him the sort of love he had with your mother, don't you?"

Maggie didn't answer, but Elizabeth hadn't really expected her to. She merely hoped she'd given the girl some food for thought.

Sonny returned then and said regretfully, "I'm sorry, Lissa, but I've got to go to the hospital for a while. Dinner will have to wait."

"That's all right, Sonny," Elizabeth immediately said. "I'll go home and wait. Maggie looks like she's getting sleepy."

She stood aside as Sonny bent to kiss Maggie's forehead.

"You go upstairs and get some rest, honey," he told his daughter, "and if you need anything, just call down to Mrs. Mullins on the intercom."

"I will, Daddy," Maggie said a little more soberly than was her wont. "But I think I'm sleepy now."

"Good. That's the best thing for you."

Maggie trudged upstairs, and Sonny walked Elizabeth to the door. Putting his arms around her, he kissed her thoroughly. When he raised his head, his eyes were glowing with humor and desire.

"I was beginning to think I was suffering withdrawal symptoms," he teased softly. "That's the first kiss I've had from you in over three days."

"But it was all the better for the wait," Elizabeth teased back, tightening her arms around his neck to hold him close.

Sonny kissed her again . . . and then again . . . and by the time he raised his head, his breathing was unsteady, as was Elizabeth's.

"I've got to go," he said, "but I'll be damned if I want to. I'd much rather be with you than listening to Mrs. Hadley complain to me that she thinks her surgeon left something that isn't supposed to be there in her abdomen."

Elizabeth burst out laughing. "You don't think she's right, do you?" she chortled.

"Of course not," Sonny said, grinning. "Mrs. Hadley would complain if God Himself had done her surgery."

After he'd helped her on with her coat, he held the lapels and drew her close to him. "I'll be by to get you when I'm through at the hospital," he said huskily. "Be ready for me."

Elizabeth swallowed, nodded and raised her mouth for another kiss, which Sonny made a slow, tantalizing one that left them both breathless again. Then Sonny put his own coat on and they walked out to their separate cars together, hand in hand.

As Sonny drove to the hospital, he was smiling and whistling. At that moment, he'd have been willing to bet his practice that before another six months had gone by, Lissa Farrell would be changing her name to Strotherton.

Elizabeth drove home thinking about Maggie. She had no doubt that she could become fond of the girl, but she also had no doubt that Maggie was the type of child who would push adults just as far as they would let her. Still, it might help smooth things over with Maggie when the girl learned that her heroine, the Vixen, and Lissa Farrell were one and the same . . . that is, if Sonny allowed the relationship to continue once he found out the same thing.

Elizabeth dressed in a feminine pale-pink and gray silk dress and when Sonny arrived to pick her up, his eyes swept over her caressingly and he gave a low whistle of appreciation.

"My beautiful Lissa," he said as he pulled her into his arms and ran his hands over her back. Then he sobered and held her gaze steadily. "You will be mine one day, Lissa. I'm convinced of it."

Elizabeth's expression was as sober as his. "Only time will tell, Sonny," she said huskily, "but I'm beginning to hope you're right."

Sonny studied her face, glad of her response, but made uneasy by the slight note of doubt in her tone. But he didn't want to deal with doubt right then. He wanted to savor being with Lissa to the exclusion of all else.

"Come on," he said, smiling. "Let's go eat before I sweep you off your feet, carry you upstairs, and ravish you unmercifully."

The thought was so appealing to Elizabeth that she had to look away in order not to give Sonny a silent invitation to carry out his threat.

By the time they'd had a leisurely meal and a bottle of wine, and had returned home, Sonny was in such a dangerously erotic mood, he was afraid to trust himself to be alone with Lissa.

Elizabeth, however, couldn't bear for him to rush off and she drew him to her father's study, got him a snifter of brandy, then sat down beside him on the leather couch to sip her own.

"Your father had an impressive medical library," Sonny said, gesturing at the book-lined walls. "How much of it have you read?"

"Quite a bit." Elizabeth smiled, reaching out to stroke the back of Sonny's neck with her fingers. The wine had put her in a reckless, amorous mood, and though she knew she was playing with fire, she couldn't resist touching Sonny.

He reached up and caught her hand, bringing it to his mouth to kiss her palm.

Elizabeth felt her body warming up, and the expression in her eyes was slumberous as Sonny looked up at her.

He found her expression too tempting to resist. Setting his brandy aside, he reached for hers and set it aside as well.

"Come here, Lissa," he said, his voice low and slightly rough. "My patience is about at an end."

As much as Elizabeth wanted to go to him, his last words made her hesitate.

Sonny made up his mind then and there that if it took every speck of willpower he had, he would create a need in Lissa that she couldn't easily dismiss. But at the same time, he had no intention of seducing her completely until he knew she could come to him without a single reservation, for fear he might lose her completely if he was too precipitate.

"Lissa, I haven't forgotten my promise," he said with soft firmness. "Come here."

Searching his face, Elizabeth believed that he hadn't forgotten, and she leaned closer, whereupon Sonny lifted her smoothly and turned her until she was lying in his lap.

"Now," he said, his voice low and purposeful, his eyes alight with a blue flame. "Let's see if I remember how to go to the brink and then get up and walk away before burning up completely."

Elizabeth felt a thrill of pleasure, spiced with a hint of fear because of the purposefulness in Sonny's expression. But she was beginning to trust him enough to dismiss the fear, and in any case, once Sonny's mouth opened over hers and his arms tightened around her, she wasn't capable of feeling anything but complete involvement in the pleasure he gave her.

Sonny kissed Lissa again and again, on her mouth, her eyelids, her cheeks, her long, lovely throat, and it was the hardest thing he'd ever done to keep remembering that his intention was to give her as much intense pleasure as she could stand while containing his own to manageable limits.

He touched her freely, boldly, as though she were already his, caressing her breasts skillfully, trying to dim his ears to the tiny gasps of excitement she gave rather than let the sound push him over the brink. He ran his palm under her dress, up over her silk-sheathed legs, between her thighs, tantalizing her with tiny, glancing touches until she was trembling and writhing in his lap.

Elizabeth was beyond thought. She craved more and more, and she was soon made frantic by Sonny's tantalizing mouth and hands, which pushed her toward a peak of excitement she'd never known before, then drifted away, frustrating her until she wanted to beg him to give her release.

At last, she heard her own voice saying the words reverberating in her mind.

"Sonny, please . . . ," she gasped, arching under the erotic stroke of his maddening hand. "Make love to me . . . make love to me, Sonny. I can't stand it anymore!"

Sonny was lost then. Sweat stood out on his brow, and his eyes held a flaming look as, in automatic compliance, he turned his body and placed Lissa on her back on the couch, then covered her body with his. She arched against him as he smothered her mouth and thrust his tongue deep within the sweet cavity behind it. And then, as he was about to stop kissing her and start undressing her, he felt her shuddering in a release of the tension he'd built up in her, and his sense-drugged mind accepted that he'd accomplished what he'd set out to do too well. Lissa had gone over the brink without him.

He held her until the shudders ceased, and then was dismayed when she clutched him tightly in her arms and burst into tears.

"Lissa . . . Lissa . . . ," he tried to soothe her, his voice slurred with his own passion. "Don't cry. It's all right, dearest. There's nothing to cry about."

Elizabeth was wrung with conflicting emotions and the tears had burst out of her with a spontaneity that surprised her as much as Sonny. She felt ashamed of her lack of control earlier and now. She felt as though she'd been horribly unfair to Sonny, first begging him to make love to her, then being unable to wait and do it right. And now the aftermath of such overwhelming passion had left her feeling too empty and shaken to make things up to him or even to control her own tears.

"Lissa . . . sweet Lissa . . . ," Sonny murmured, shifting to lie beside her and cuddle her close. "It happens, darling. You know that. Don't feel . . ."

But Elizabeth was shaking her head. It had never happened to her before, and she didn't feel up to explaining why it hadn't.

Sonny gave an inner sigh, interpreting Lissa's gesture to mean she didn't want to talk about what had happened. He ached from head to foot, but he was aware he'd brought this particular sort of pain on himself, and there was little likelihood of getting the chance to ease it now.

So he simply held Lissa and stroked her back comfortingly and waited for her sobs to stop and his own desire to subside.

Then, with her face muffled against his neck, she said, "I'm sorry, Sonny. I'm so ashamed of myself."

Sonny frowned and drew back slightly, trying to see her face, but she wouldn't look at him. "God, Lissa, there's nothing to be ashamed of!" he protested with such gentleness in his voice that Elizabeth felt even more ashamed. "What happened was perfectly normal. If any apologies are necessary, I'm the one who should make them."

"But I should have waited!" Elizabeth wailed softly, then immediately shook her head. "No, I should have let you go home instead of insisting we come in here," she added miserably, and buried her face in his neck again.

Sonny grimaced at this indication that Lissa still had a divided mind.

"No, Lissa," he said quietly. "I should have remembered that a man who's been celibate for two years hasn't got any business testing his mettle against a woman as lovely as you. I was so determined to make you want me that I went too far and pushed you over the brink. You didn't have a chance against what I put you through, and you don't owe me any apologies."

Elizabeth felt marginally better. "Really?" she asked, her voice muffled.

"Really," Sonny assured her, smiling with somewhat rueful grimness. He drew his head back, and this time Elizabeth met his reassuring look.

"Have you really been celibate for two years?" she asked quietly.

Sonny nodded calmly, and Elizabeth fell a little bit more in love with him. "I suppose that's a contributing factor in my lack of control," he said wryly, "though it really isn't an excuse."

Isn't it? Elizabeth thought silently, thinking that two years of celibacy explained a lot about Sonny's ambivalent attitude the night he'd come back to her dressing room. He had been attracted to her, even as the Vixen, but when she'd put on her act to drive him away, then kissed him, his body and his head had been in severe conflict.

"I'd better go, Lissa," Sonny said, hugging her for a second before he sat up and pulled her up with him. "I think we'll have a better time to do it right one of these days . . ." He paused, smiling at her, and added, ". . . and if I'm lucky, that time will come soon. But I want it to come when you're ready, not because I seduced you. I want it to be right as much as you do."

After he'd put on his coat, Sonny drew her to him and simply held her for a long moment. "Are you all right now about what happened, Lissa?" he asked quietly.

Elizabeth hesitated, then nodded. She wasn't all right exactly, but the least she could do was reassure Sonny that she was.

"Good. Then kiss me good night and I'll call you tomorrow and we'll make plans to do something." He left her with the sweetness of his kiss on her lips.

But the next day, Sonny had emergencies with two of his patients and they didn't have a chance to see one another that day or for several days after that, because Elizabeth was caught up with medical school and had little energy for anything else.

Sonny understood. He'd been there himself. So he remained reasonably content with telephone calls for a while. But finally his patience broke and he was waiting in Elizabeth's driveway for her when she arrived home about seven o'clock one night after having spent time in the library.

"Sonny!" she said as she got out of her car. "What's wrong? Is Maggie all right?"

"Maggie's fine," Sonny drawled as he walked her to her front door, "but her father is on the verge of a collapse."

Elizabeth looked at him in alarm. "What is it?" she asked fearfully. "Have you been working too hard? Are you sick? What . . ."

"Whoa." Sonny held up a hand, then took the key from her fingers, opened the door, escorted her inside, then pulled her into his arms.

"It's those damned withdrawal symptoms again," he teased softly as he nuzzled her cheek. "I have to have some time with you or . . ."

"Sonny!" Elizabeth drew back, a mock glare on her face. "How could you worry me like that when there's nothing wrong?!"

Sonny was pleased rather than discouraged. "Were you worried, Lissa?" he asked blandly. And before she could answer, he added, "And it's a matter of interpretation whether anything's wrong or not.

When I can't kiss you and hold you and see your beautiful face, something's wrong, believe me!"

Elizabeth smiled then and as Sonny took her mouth, she discovered she'd missed him more than she'd had time to acknowledge, and she eagerly returned his kiss. So eagerly, in fact, that Sonny's sense of humor fled, to be replaced by an upsurge of desire he could barely control.

He drew back and Elizabeth's expression made his heart thud in his chest, it was so soft and inviting.

Then the telephone began ringing, and Sonny didn't know whether to be glad or sorry. He didn't know how much longer he could take the frustration he lived with day and night these days.

Elizabeth went to the kitchen to answer the phone and Sonny followed her.

"Hello?" she said into the receiver, hoping it wasn't Danny since Sonny could hear her side of the conversation.

"Lissa, is my Dad there?" Maggie asked excitedly.

"Why, yes, he is, Maggie. Do you need to talk to him?"

"Yes, please," Maggie answered.

Wondering what had Maggie so excited, Elizabeth gestured at Sonny. "It's Maggie," she informed him as he came to take the phone. And when Sonny grimaced at the way his daughter had tracked him down, Elizabeth pressed her palm against his cheek. "Be nice," she whispered, before handing him the phone.

"Yes, Maggie, what is it?" Sonny said.

Elizabeth didn't listen to his side of the conversation. She was too involved in the old familiar, and most unwelcome, dilemma about what to do. Things were heating up between her and Sonny to the point where she knew she couldn't delay telling him the truth much longer. It wasn't fair to him. It wasn't even fair to herself.

"Oh, hell, Maggie . . . ," she heard Sonny say, and when she glanced over at him, she saw that he was looking grimly disgusted.

"I know I told you you could have what you wanted for your birthday, honey, but . . ."

Sonny fell silent as Maggie evidently chattered on, and Elizabeth's curiosity began to surface as she saw the conflict reflected on Sonny's face.

Finally, she saw him lift his shoulders in a gesture of fatalism, and heard him say, "All right . . . all right, Maggie. I'll do it this once. Only because it's your birthday."

When he hung up, Elizabeth looked at him questioningly. "Is today Maggie's birthday?" she asked.

"No, it's Saturday," Sonny replied grimly, "and I've just promised her I'll take her to one of those idiotic rock concerts to celebrate it."

Elizabeth felt a little chill go through her. "Oh?" she said casually. "Who is it she wants to go see?"

"The Fearsome Foursome . . . Freaky Foursome . . . some damned nonsensical name like that. All I'm really certain of is that the group's got a lead singer named the Vixen, and Maggie's got a crush on her for some reason that's beyond me. The woman's completely worthless!"

Sonny raked his hand through his hair, aware that his vehement resistance to Maggie's desire to go to the rock concert now went beyond his fear that the group would influence his daughter negatively. He had his own reasons for not wanting to see the Vixen again. He didn't want to be reminded that he'd actually been attracted to the woman. Now that he'd met Lissa, he felt ashamed that he'd been so foolish. Lissa was worth a thousand cheap singers like the Vixen.

Elizabeth felt frozen by Sonny's words. "What do you mean, she's 'worthless'?" she asked tonelessly.

Sonny looked at her in surprise. He didn't want to admit to Lissa that he'd met the Vixen, especially that he'd actually kissed her!

"Have you seen her?" he evaded answering directly. "All that makeup and the god-awful costumes she wears? Should I be pleased that Maggie thinks she's wonderful?"

Elizabeth stared at him. "It's just part of the act, Sonny," she said quietly.

Sonny gave her an impatient look. "I don't think so. That might be true of some singers of that type, but not her. I think she's as cheap as she looks."

Elizabeth felt her numbness dissolving into anger. "How can you be sure, Sonny?" she asked recklessly. "Do you know this woman?"

Sonny was faced with either telling an out-and-out lie, which he didn't want to do, or evading the question.

"What difference does it make?" He chose evasion. "I've promised Maggie I'll take her, and I will, but I'd just as soon not talk about it anymore, except to ask you if you'll come with us."

"I can't, Sonny," she said flatly. "I have too much studying to do, and besides, it's Maggie's birthday. Let her have a good time without feeling that I'm in the way."

Though Sonny was actually relieved that Lissa wasn't coming with him—he hadn't relished the thought of sitting beside her watching the Vixen and remembering what had happened between them—he was disturbed by her tone of voice. Did Maggie's attitude hurt Lissa more than he'd realized?

"Lissa, Maggie's bringing a couple of her girlfriends along with her, so I don't think she'd mind if you came as well."

Elizabeth shook her head. "I still have that studying to do," she said, and added, "As a matter of fact, I have a lot of studying to do tonight, Sonny, so I hope you don't mind, but I ought to get to it."

Something about Lissa's attitude disturbed Sonny, but he decided she was merely reacting to his showing up here needing to hold and kiss her. No doubt, she was afraid if he stayed, the same thing would happen between them that had happened the last time they'd been together . . . as it very well might. His control was fraying ever more rapidly.

He came to her and pulled her up into his arms, but she didn't relax against him, and she wouldn't meet his eyes.

"Lissa, I'm trying to be patient," he said softly. "I really am. It's just that . . ."

Lissa shook her head impatiently. She felt estranged from him, and she didn't want to talk about what had happened the last time they'd been together. Not when he seemed almost a stranger to her right now.

"It's all right," she said. "I understand. But I do have to study, Sonny. I'm sorry, but I want to do my best."

Sonny wished she would look at him, and when she didn't, he placed his fingers under her chin and turned her face up to his.

Elizabeth forced a blank expression onto her face.

Sonny knew something was wrong, but he didn't know what to do about it. "Lissa, I'm trying," he repeated. It was all he could think of to say.

"I know." Elizabeth nodded absently, then, in order to make Sonny cease his intent inspection of her face and go away, she lifted her lips to his and kissed him.

She was relieved when the kiss seemed to convince Sonny that she was all right.

"I'll call you tomorrow," he said as he shrugged into his coat. "And Lissa," he added, smiling at her warmly, "I wouldn't want you to slack off on your studies, but if you'll take the advice of someone who's been there, it helps to get completely away from the books occasionally. You come back fresher."

"I'll keep that in mind." Elizabeth nodded. "Maybe when I'm more used to all of it, I'll be able to take things easier."

"I'm sure you will," Sonny agreed. Then he kissed her lightly before heading for the door. "Good night, Lissa," he said caressingly.

"Good night, Sonny," Elizabeth echoed his tone, but when he was gone, her expression tautened. It had hurt more than she would ever have believed possible to hear Sonny describe the Vixen as "worthless," and his attitude hadn't encouraged her in the least that when the time came for him to know the truth, he was going to accept it with an open mind.

And Sonny went home feeling angry and dejected, wondering if he was losing Lissa Farrell to the other man he feared existed . . . a man who might not be making the same sort of mistake Sonny had the last time he'd been with her.

CHAPTER THIRTEEN

"Oh, God, Darla, no! Anytime but now!"

Darla's voice over the phone became impatient. "Lissa, I can't help it. They can't stop the bleeding, and Mom's got to have that operation right away. I've got to go to her. Surely you understand?"

Lissa felt trapped, but, of course, she did understand, and she felt ashamed of adding to Darla's worries by her poor reaction to the news that she was going to have to take Darla's place for the concert that weekend. She wouldn't have been particularly happy about the situation at any time, but Sonny and Maggie would be going to this concert!

"I'm sorry, Darla," she apologized sincerely. "I just wasn't thinking. Is there anything else I can do to help? Do you have enough money?"

"Yes, Danny gave me an advance," Darla answered, "and he wants to speak to you now, okay?"

"Yes, all right. And Darla," she added, "I'll be praying for you and your mother."

"Thanks, Lissa," Darla said gratefully. "You're a real friend."

Then Danny came onto the line. "We'll be back in town Thursday night, Lissa," he said. "Can you skip classes Friday to rehearse?"

"No, Danny," Lissa said firmly. "I'll rehearse with you Friday night and Saturday, and that will have to do."

To her surprise, Danny didn't give her any trouble about her decision. "All right, then," he agreed. "The guys and I will rest up Friday, and we'll get to it when you get home that evening."

When they rang off, Elizabeth slumped in her chair, feeling exhausted. Then she realized it wasn't really physical fatigue that was getting to her, but the emotional strain of practicing deception. She couldn't remember ever feeling like this in her life until Danny had first asked her to help him out over a year ago and she had been torn between her loyalty to him and her fear that helping him would damage her own chances to have a successful career as a physician.

The tears with Sonny the other night should have told her something about her state of mind, but she was only now realizing how high the cost of deception could be to someone like her who found lies and subterfuge so abhorrent.

Elizabeth sat up straight, feeling disgusted with herself for her first reaction to Darla's news. All she had thought about was that Sonny might somehow discover it was she up on the stage instead of Darla, and the disgust he had for the Vixen would then transfer to Elizabeth Farrell.

"And what if it does?" she told herself fiercely. "After I explain, if he loves me, he'll understand and it won't matter. If he doesn't love me and can't understand, there's no future for us anyway!"

The time had come to tell Sonny the truth, and Elizabeth knew she had to do it before the concert. There was no question that Sonny's reaction would be worse if he discovered the truth by accident rather than from her own lips.

She was nervous, but she also felt a sense of relief as she reached for the telephone to call Sonny to ask him to come over. She had planned to study, but for once, her studies could wait.

She was so keyed up to act at last that her disappointment was acute when Mrs. Mullins informed her that Sonny had left for Florida that afternoon. His retired father had had chest pains and was in the hospital for tests, and his mother had asked him to come. Maggie was with him.

"He would have called you, but you were in classes," Mrs. Mullins explained, "and he asked me to call you, but your line has been busy. I was just about to try again when you rang up."

"Yes, I'm sorry," Elizabeth said absently. "Well, thank you, Mrs.

Mullins, and if Dr. Strotherton calls in, tell him I'm sorry about his father."

"Of course," Mrs. Mullins agreed, "but he may call you directly."

I hope so, Elizabeth thought rather forlornly. Even though she had no intention of explaining anything to Sonny over the phone, especially when he must be frantic with worry about his father, she longed to hear his voice and give him what comfort she could.

It was the following evening before Sonny had a chance to call Elizabeth, and he was disappointed when she didn't answer.

She's probably at the library, he thought wryly, feeling both proud of her dedication to her studies, and yet a little resentful that they took so much of her time. *Well, I'll call her when Maggie and I get home tomorrow evening and tell her the good news about Dad,* he decided as he hung up and returned to his father's bedroom. The chest pains had been indigestion and his father was back home.

But the next evening, which was Friday, when Sonny again tried to call Elizabeth, she was at Danny's small studio with the rest of the Foursome rehearsing for her next appearance as the Vixen.

Sonny kept calling all that evening, and finally went to bed around midnight, very much afraid of where she might be.

The next morning, Lissa didn't hear the phone when Sonny called before leaving for the hospital to make his rounds. She'd been up until 3:00 A.M. rehearsing, and her fatigue from the hours she'd been putting in on her studies lately, as well as the emotional strain she'd been under, had left her tired to the point of exhaustion.

Therefore, it was Danny who answered the phone at six o'clock that morning, and the grogginess in his voice made it obvious to Sonny that the man answering Lissa's phone had slept there the previous evening. The implication devastated him.

"Hello?" Danny repeated irritably when Sonny didn't respond to his first greeting. "Who's there?"

His face white, his eyes reflecting the pain and fury he felt, Sonny grated, "I'd like to speak to Elizabeth Farrell, please."

Danny was tired and not thinking too clearly, and he automatically assumed the man on the phone was a fan of Lissa's . . . or rather the

Vixen's. It had happened before. A legitimate call would have come at a decent hour, and Danny, feeling tired and irritable, was in no mood to put up with a nuisance call this early. Therefore, he answered sarcastically in a way that wasn't a lie, but might discourage the man if he fancied himself a would-be suitor of Lissa's.

"Oh, you would, would you? Well, forget it, buddy. I kept her up late last night, and I have plans for her when she wakes up this morning. Now bug off and let us get some sleep, all right?" And he slammed the phone down in Sonny's ear, turned over in bed, jerked the covers up over his shoulder, and went back to sleep.

Sonny, feeling like he'd just been punched in the stomach with a giant fist and wanted to hit back, instead hung up on the phone on his end and left his house, grim-faced, to make his rounds. He was too dedicated a doctor to neglect his patients in order to go punch out the man who'd just informed him that he was in bed with the woman Sonny loved . . . or to pursue a woman who apparently had finally made up her mind which man she wanted.

"Danny, it will only take a minute," Lissa insisted as they left the house to rehearse later that morning. "And it's important. It's not even out of the way!"

Elizabeth knew how tense Danny got on the day of a performance, but she was in no mood to cater to his nerves for the time being. After having called Sonny's house and being informed by Mrs. Mullins that Sonny was back but had gone to the hospital, and knowing she would have no time to talk to Sonny before the performance that evening, Lissa had decided to leave him a note. She couldn't explain anything in the note other than to say she desperately needed to talk to him, but she could at least do that much.

"All right, all right," Danny growled, and grudgingly headed for the Strotherton houschold.

Danny and Jay sat in the black Ferrari out in the driveway while Elizabeth, note in hand, ran up to the front door and rang the bell.

When Mrs. Mullins answered the door, Elizabeth thrust the note at her. "Please give this to Sonny when he gets home, Mrs. Mullins," she said. "I won't be able to talk to him today, and I know he's taking

Maggie out this evening, but I do need to talk to him as soon as possible . . . if not later on tonight, then in the morning."

"Of course, Ms. Farrell," Mrs. Mullins replied as she took the note. "I'll give it to him just as soon as he gets home."

"Thanks," Elizabeth said gratefully. "Good-bye, Mrs. Mullins," she added as she turned to run back to the car, leaving Sonny's housekeeper to stare curiously at the black Ferrari, the handsome young black-haired man behind the wheel, and another man in the backseat.

That afternoon, Sonny listened as Mrs. Mullins handed him Elizabeth's note and innocently described the car and the driver who'd brought her to the house.

"Thank you, Mrs. Mullins," he said coldly, startling his housekeeper with his tone and the icy look in his blue eyes.

"You're welcome, Doctor," she said hesitantly and quickly made herself scarce, wondering what he was so angry about.

Sonny took the note out of the envelope, unfolded it, and read the brief message in a coldly cynical frame of mind:

> "Sonny, I have something very important to talk to you about as soon as possible. I know it will be late when you get home from the concert tonight, and if you'd prefer, it can wait until tomorrow morning, but if you can see me tonight, I won't mind how late it is. It's *important,* Sonny.
>
> "I'm so glad your father's all right, and I'm glad you're back.
> Love, Lissa"

Sonny's lip curled as he read the last sentence. How glad could Lissa be to have him back when she'd spent the night in her lover's arms? Probably, she just wanted to tell him she wouldn't be seeing him anymore.

No thanks, Lissa, he thought as he violently tore the note in two and threw it in his wastebasket. *I don't need to hear your news in person. I've already gotten the message from your lover.*

He was almost finished dressing for the concert when Maggie, clad in a semi-punk outfit Sonny normally would have eyed with complete disfavor, came into his bedroom looking as happy as the cat who'd caught the canary. When she caught sight of her father's face, however, her expression dissolved.

"Daddy, what's the matter?" she asked anxiously. "Is Granddad sick again?"

Sonny made the effort to smile reassuringly at her. "No, Granddad's fine, honey. Something's bothering me but it's nothing for you to worry about."

Maggie looked doubtful, then curious.

"Does it have anything to do with Lissa Farrell?" she asked.

Sonny hesitated. The wound was still too raw for him to want to talk about it, but he decided he might as well make Maggie happy with his news. It was her birthday, after all.

"Yes," he nodded, turning away so that Maggie couldn't see his expression. "I won't be seeing her anymore, Maggie."

Maggie brightened immediately, and was about to ask her Dad why, but then she caught sight of his face in the mirror. The pain in his eyes made her think about his side of things. In fact, she'd been thinking about his side of things off and on since she'd had that talk with Lissa, but she hadn't been willing until now to accept that her dad really cared so much for Lissa.

"I . . . well, I'm sorry, Dad," she said awkwardly.

Sonny turned around to look at her, his expression grim. "No, you're not, Maggie. We both know you couldn't be happier that Lissa's not going to be around anymore. Don't pretend otherwise."

Maggie wriggled uncomfortably. "Well, I guess you're right in a way," she admitted. "It's just that you look so unhappy, Daddy . . . and I don't like you to be hurt."

Sonny gradually relaxed, and he came to take Maggie in his arms. "Don't worry about me, honey," he said quietly as he held her close. "I'm all right." *At least, I will be eventually,* Sonny added silently. "Now, let me finish getting ready so I can get you and your friends to that concert on time."

Maggie smiled and kissed him on the cheek before she left him, and Sonny felt very grateful that he had her love. It felt like that was all he did have for the moment.

* * *

Despite the fact that there hadn't been much advance notice for the concert, the hall was packed with teenagers and college students. As well as being reluctant to see the Vixen again, Sonny felt somewhat out of place among the rowdy group. But since he'd felt Maggie and her friends were too young to attend such a concert on their own, he was resigned to getting through the evening. He did wish, however, that their seats weren't quite so good, because there was every chance the Vixen would spot him and Maggie. Should that happen, Maggie, of course, would be thrilled. Sonny's attitude was the opposite. He didn't want the Vixen to think he had come here particularly to see her and, as a result, perhaps embarrass him in front of his daughter.

You've got enough trouble without looking for more, Sonny, he told himself savagely. *Chances are, the Vixen can't see the audience clearly because of the lights, and anyway, she's probably forgotten you exist.*

Backstage, Elizabeth nervously finished putting on her makeup, taking more care with it than usual because tonight, of all nights, she didn't want to be recognized . . . not until she'd had a chance to talk to Sonny and explain things to him.

Danny put his head in the door and said, "Hurry it up, Lissa . . . let's go," before he withdrew again.

Elizabeth stood up and looked at herself in the mirror. The only costume that wasn't being cleaned or mended had been the lavender camisole and dark purple miniskirt, and she was wearing the purple boa that went with them, black patterned hose and purple heels. So naturally she was also wearing the same lavender wig she'd worn the night Sonny had come back to her dressing room and kissed her. But her grimace at herself in the mirror said clearly that if there'd been other choices, she would gladly have taken them.

"Come *on*, Lissa!" Jay yelled at her from the door of her dressing room, and Elizabeth grabbed up her tambourine and followed him to the wings.

As the four of them waited for the backup musicians to finish the song they were playing as a warmup, Lissa stood where she could see

160

part of the audience without being seen herself, and she blanched when she saw Sonny, Maggie, and two other girls Maggie's age in the center row, only a few aisles back from the stage.

She would have given a lot for them to have been seated farther away, but since there was nothing she could do about it, she told herself not to worry. Surely her disguise would protect her one more time.

Then the backup musicians were playing the Foursome's introduction, and Lissa allowed habit to guide her as she slithered onto the stage, thinking it was going to be a very long night.

The audience around him, as well as Maggie and her friends, was erupting into wild cheers and screams as the Foursome came running on stage to the accompaniment of throbbing music, but Sonny sat very still, his eyes focused only on the Vixen.

She was as wild-looking as ever, and he mentally shook his head, wondering how he'd ever been attracted to such a woman. As he realized she was wearing the same lavender wig and purple lipstick she'd been wearing the night he'd kissed her, he winced inwardly. Had he really been that hard up? he wondered incredulously.

But then a strange thought occurred to him. The Vixen might dress like a tramp, and she might have behaved like a tramp the night he'd visited her in her dressing room, but as he recalled the way she'd acted during the visit he and Maggie had paid her together, he realized she had made an effort to be a good influence on his daughter. So maybe she wasn't as bad as he'd thought. At least, she was on her best behavior when it counted the most.

On the other hand, Lissa Farrell, who was outwardly every inch a lady, obviously had enough libido for two women, and no compunction about keeping two men on the string at the same time . . . at least for a while.

Sonny frowned, feeling hurt and confused and thoroughly unhappy.

Lissa sang along with the group, and though she tried not to make it obvious, she found her eyes returning again and again to Sonny. She was looking at him when he frowned, and seeing the unhappy expression on his face, her heart went out to him. Maybe he'd had more bad news about his father. She wanted very badly to comfort him and erase that terrible unhappiness from his face . . . badly enough to take a risk.

When the first number was over, she caught Danny's arm as he was about to make his introductory remarks and tiptoed to whisper in his ear. Danny frowned, but when Elizabeth gave him a pleading look, he finally shrugged and nodded, then grabbed the microphone.

"Hey, everybody!" he yelled at the audience, giving them his most charming grin. "It's always good to be back in Boston, my own hometown!"

The audience cheered enthusiastically, and when they calmed down, Danny said, "Well, you guys didn't come here to hear me talk, so let's get to it!" The cheer came again and Danny held out a hand to Lissa, who joined him at the microphone. "Let's hear it for the Vixen!" Danny yelled, to the accompaniment of another swelling cheer.

Danny made a gesture at the band, and mouthed a title to them, which caused Jay and Jerry to look surprised. But they shrugged and went into the introduction of "You're the Only Man for Me," and Lissa swayed to the music until the audience had quieted down enough for her to begin singing.

Sonny had stiffened as he caught the first few notes of the song and realized what they were going to play, and then he froze entirely as Lissa stared directly at him and began to half-sing, half-speak the words, her voice huskily sincere. "I lie awake all night remembering . . . my heart and body find no peace nor ease. I want a man who loved me once with everything . . . then left me lonely when I somehow failed to please."

A welter of impressions and emotions raced through Sonny's mind as he stared back at the Vixen and accepted that she was singing that song to him and him alone. He couldn't believe it at first. One kiss surely couldn't inspire the kind of feeling the Vixen was displaying in her eyes and voice.

He also had trouble accepting how very moved he felt as he listened and stared and . . .

Sonny's gaze sharpened as he focused on the Vixen's eyes again, and at the same time strained harder to hear. *Hell, I've only seen her twice,* he thought, bewildered by his impression that there was something a great deal more familiar about the Vixen than should be warranted by their two brief meetings.

Elizabeth went into the chorus then, but instead of singing it the way she normally did, she spoke it directly to Sonny. Later, she would wonder how she could have behaved so foolishly. But at this moment, everything in her was focused on making him understand that there was truth in the words, and that he should trust her to mean what she was singing to him.

"Oh, Lord, what do I do . . . how do I make him see . . . that he's the only man for me . . . the *only* man for me."

As Sonny listened to Elizabeth speak the words in her normal voice, something clicked in his mind, but at first he wouldn't accept it. He sat stunned, totally unable to believe that what his senses were telling him could be true. Those large violet eyes holding his own were Lissa's eyes . . . the voice was too familiar to deny . . . but it just couldn't be Lissa up on that stage! It couldn't be!

The expression of shock on Sonny's face brought Elizabeth to her senses, and she felt a cold chilling shock of her own. How could she have been so foolish? she wondered in a panic as she broke eye contact with Sonny, turned her back on him, and continued the song automatically, hardly knowing what she was singing.

Danny saw the change in Elizabeth's manner and heard the faint quaver in her voice. Since he was playing the guitar instead of the piano, he moved up beside her to catch her eye. He was alarmed when she gazed blankly back at him, and to cover the growing faintness of her voice, he joined in and made it a duet.

Elizabeth felt the burning intensity of Danny's will focused on her, and was grateful that his joining in the song gave her a chance to gather her poise again. After a moment, her voice grew stronger and she could see Danny relax as she slowly got herself back together.

Meanwhile, Sonny looked from Lissa to Danny, realized that the voice on the phone that morning matched the one this young man had used in his introduction, and remembered Mrs. Mullins's description of the man who had driven Lissa to his house that morning. And slowly, his mind and heart filled with rage . . . a type of rage he'd never experienced before and which left him shaken. Lissa had not only kept her identity as the Vixen from him . . . she'd been involved romantically all along with her singing partner!

He was on his feet and heading for the aisle before he was even aware of his own intentions.

Elizabeth caught his movement out of the corner of her eye, and her voice faltered again as she watched Sonny stride out of the auditorium. His manner spelled out clearly what his departure meant.

Neither Sonny nor Elizabeth thought to look at Maggie. But if they had, they would have seen a look of shock on her young face as vivid as her father's had been. She watched her father's progress to the auditorium doors, and when he was out of sight, she returned her attention to the Vixen, and silently mouthed the words, "Lissa Farrell? *Lissa?!*"

And for the duration of the concert, two bright, sparkling ice-blue eyes eagerly watched every move the Vixen made and listened carefully to every word the Vixen sang.

It was not the best performance the Vixen had given by any means. But while Danny Farrell was thoroughly displeased by his sister's lack of attention and the mistakes she made, Maggie Strotherton couldn't have been happier, and her applause was long and loudly enthusiastic when the Vixen took her last bow.

CHAPTER FOURTEEN

The moment they'd dropped off her friends and she and her father were alone in the car, Maggie rushed into speech.

"Oh, Daddy, I can't believe it!" she chortled. When Sonny frowned at her, not understanding what she was talking about and not really in a mood to learn, she chattered on. "You didn't know, did you? I wonder why she didn't tell us? If she had, I'd never have acted badly to her. I'd have welcomed her with open arms!"

Sonny then realized that Maggie had discovered Lissa and the Vixen were one and the same, and his expression tautened.

"No, I didn't know, Maggie," he said harshly, "but now that I do, I'm very grateful Lissa and I are through."

Maggie stared at her father in dismay. "Oh, Daddy, you can't mean that!" she protested. "Are you mad at her because she didn't tell us? But she must have had a good reason, Daddy, if you'll just let her explain! Listen, let's call her when we get home. I want to tell her . . ."

Maggie broke off and drew back at the look on Sonny's face. She'd never seen him look like that, and she didn't like it at all!

"Maggie, I don't want to talk about Lissa Farrell or the Vixen!" he grated in a voice he'd never used with her before. "It's over, and that's all there is to it! Now, hush!"

Maggie's mouth was open in shock, but she quickly closed it. Her father's manner was such that it didn't even occur to her to disobey him. But as she huddled in her seat close to tears, she realized her Dad hadn't forbidden her to talk to Lissa herself. He'd just said *he* didn't want to talk about her.

Maggie's tears quickly dried up as she began to think. Soon, she was hiding a smile, which faded as she glanced over at her father's harsh expression. Her own expression grew resentful as she wondered why it was parents never did anything right! First, her Dad had tried to foist Lissa Farrell on her when she didn't want to have anything to do with her, and now he was depriving her of a chance to have the Vixen as a stepmother! It just wasn't fair!

After the concert, Elizabeth didn't even bother to remove her makeup and costume, nor did she wait to receive the dressing down she knew Danny wanted to give her. Instead, she grabbed her coat and headed straight for the stagedoor where she had the attendant find her a taxi.

Forty-five minutes later, she was sitting on the edge of her bed staring at the phone, wondering what was the use of putting herself through the pain of calling Sonny. For him, it was over between them. She knew that as certainly as though he'd told her so.

But he's still due an explanation, and I deserve the chance to give him one, she thought leadenly, and dialed his number.

Sonny and Maggie were just coming through the front door when the phone began to ring. Sonny ignored it. If it was a patient, his answering service would pick it up.

Maggie, however, raced to the kitchen and grabbed the wall phone. "Hello?" she said breathlessly.

"Maggie," Elizabeth said with false calm, "this is Lissa. May I speak to your father?"

Maggie heard Sonny come into the room, and she glanced at him doubtfully. "Just a minute," she said to Lissa, then covered the mouthpiece with her hand. "Daddy, it's Lissa," she said innocently. "She wants to talk to you."

Sonny tensed his jaw and gave his daughter a hard look. "Well, I don't want to talk to her, Maggie," he grated. "Tell her that."

He turned and walked away, and Maggie grimaced at his back before lifting her hand away from the mouthpiece.

"Lissa, he won't talk to you," she almost whispered in case Sonny hadn't gone far and could hear. "He's really mad, Lissa," Maggie said breathlessly. "I've never seen him like this." She rushed on before Lissa could reply, demanding, "Lissa, why didn't you tell us you were the Vixen? I would have been thrilled!"

Elizabeth grimaced. "I know you would have been, Maggie," she answered with that false calm in her voice again. "But I was only the Vixen for a while, and I won't be the Vixen again after tonight. I was only helping out tonight because the new Vixen couldn't be there."

Maggie's expression was confused. "But weren't you the Vixen who gave me her autograph?"

"Yes." Lissa sighed. She was on the verge of tears. "Listen, Maggie, I'm tired and upset," she said, hanging on to her control. "If your father will let you talk to me, I'll take you for a Coke someday soon and explain everything. Meanwhile, I have a favor to ask of you."

"Okay, Lissa," Maggie said, wide-eyed with confusion, but still excited that the *Vixen* was actually talking to her like this!

"I know it will be hard not to tell your friends about this, but I'd like it very much if you'd keep this our secret for now. Will you?"

"Sure!" Maggie said enthusiastically, thrilled to be having a secret with the Vixen.

"Thanks, honey," Elizabeth said tiredly. "I'll talk to you soon."

After hanging up the phone, Elizabeth lay back on her bed, covered her eyes with her arm, and let the tears flow silently down her face.

Maggie raced upstairs to find her diary, thinking that for once, she had something really exciting to write in it. This was the best birthday she ever remembered having! But it would have been an even better birthday if her dad would stop being so mad just because the Vixen hadn't told him who she really was. Parents could be so silly!

Thirty minutes later, as she was scribbling away in her diary, Sonny came into her room, and in a voice wearier than Maggie had ever heard him use, said, "Good night, honey," and he bent to kiss her forehead, then straightened and started to walk away.

Maggie couldn't hold back on asking permission to talk to Lissa.

"She wants to explain, Daddy," she finished making her request in an anxious, sober voice. "Please let me see her."

Sonny stared at his daughter thoughtfully for a moment, then shook his head, and Maggie's heart plunged at the look she saw in his eyes.

"There's no point in it, Maggie," he said in a voice Maggie knew better than to argue with. "Let it go." He started out the door, then paused and looked at Maggie again, and now his expression was pained and angry. "And for God's sake, Maggie, do me the kindness not to play any of your Foursome albums when I'm home! I've heard enough of that junk to last me a lifetime!"

Sonny turned and walked out, shutting the door of her bedroom with such a bang that Maggie involuntarily jumped. Her lower lip trembled, and tears came to her eyes for a moment, before a stubborn expression replaced them and she began to glare at the closed door of her bedroom instead.

"Parents!" she muttered scornfully. "And they keep telling us that we're the ones who are too immature to run our own lives!"

A week later, as Elizabeth drove to a shopping mall to meet Maggie and give her an explanation, she wondered wryly why Sonny had agreed to let his daughter meet with her. Didn't he fear that a worthless tramp like the Vixen might corrupt his offspring?

She quickly turned her mind away from Sonny, however, as she had been having to do for the last week. Thinking of him brought her nothing but such intense pain, she couldn't bear it, and she was unutterably grateful that she had her studies to keep her mind otherwise occupied.

Of course, this meeting with Maggie would be almost as painful as seeing Sonny himself, but it couldn't be helped. Maggie had been calling her practically every day asking to see her.

When she arrived at the restaurant, her first glance at Maggie's ice-blue eyes, so like Sonny's, assured Lissa that she hadn't been wrong in thinking this interview was going to be painful. She didn't look at Maggie any more than she could help it as they greeted one another, then bought soft drinks and sat at a table.

As Maggie waited with wide-eyed curiosity for Lissa to begin, Lissa took a deep breath and got what she had to say out as rapidly as possible, tactfully leaving out the part about Sonny coming to her dressing room in New York that time. She was grateful that Maggie listened carefully and didn't once interrupt. When she was done with her explanation, she looked at the girl and shrugged. "So now you know why I didn't want you to tell anyone about me, Maggie. But I won't hold you to it if you'd rather I didn't. That's a lot to ask of you, I know."

Maggie thought a moment, then shrugged herself. "Yeah, it'll be kind of hard not to tell my friends, but I think you're right, Lissa."

Lissa looked at Maggie with surprise and the girl grimaced. "Well, my dad didn't like the Freaky Foursome even before he got to know you, so I guess a lot of other doctors like him would be just as stuffy about it."

Elizabeth smiled ruefully. "That's what I've always been afraid of," she said unnecessarily. Then she changed her smile to a special one for Maggie and added, "Thanks, Maggie. I appreciate your understanding."

Maggie smiled back, then her gaze became curious again. "Well, I don't really understand, you know." When Lissa raised her brows in a questioning manner, Maggie shook her head. "Listen, Lissa, if I could be the Vixen, I sure wouldn't trade it in to be a boring old doctor! That's crazy!"

Elizabeth's smile broadened, then she began to laugh, the first time she'd done so all week.

"Maybe I am crazy, honey," she agreed. "But I don't think so. I'll leave music to my brother, Danny, and stick to my studies. I'm a lot happier that way and so is he."

At that, Maggie looked eager. "Can I meet your brother, Danny, sometime, Lissa?" she begged. "And the rest of the Foursome," she added quickly. "The new Vixen, too?"

Elizabeth nodded her head firmly. "Anytime they're in town, and your dad says it's all right, you can not only meet them, I'll have you over for dinner," she agreed. "But right now," she added wryly, "I've got to do some studying or I'll never get to be a boring old doctor."

The two of them laughed together and a few minutes later they parted with a hug at the entrance to the mall. As Elizabeth walked away, she was feeling a lot better than she'd expected to and for the first time, she began to believe what Darla kept telling her : . . that her life would one day be peaceful and pleasant again, instead of filled with the loneliness of losing the first man she'd ever loved.

When Sonny came home that night, he was depressed, as was usual for him these days. After his anger at Lissa had faded enough that he could think straight, he'd been able to admit to himself that it was his contemptuous attitude toward the Vixen from the moment they'd met that had prevented Lissa from telling him the truth about herself. And because of that, and, of course, her prior relationship with her singing partner, she hadn't wanted to get involved with Sonny, but he had insisted, thinking he could win her away from the rival he'd suspected existed. But the rival had won.

Sonny didn't know why Lissa hadn't told him straight out about the other man, and he still doubted she could love that man wholeheartedly when she'd responded to him, Sonny, the way she had. But maybe rock singers were accustomed to juggling more than one relationship at a time. Or maybe the other man had objected to her desire to be a doctor instead of his singing partner. Sonny wondered if the man had won on that score, too.

As he opened the back door and came into his house, the sound of Lissa singing "You're the Only Man for Me" greeted his ears, and he was abruptly furious with Maggie. Damn it, hadn't he asked her not to play that album when he was around? She knew he normally got home about this time!

Sonny strode to the family room and paused in the doorway. Maggie was sitting on the floor in front of the stereo set with her back to him, listening intently to the music.

"Maggie!" Sonny barked and when Maggie jerked and turned to face him, he strode toward her, making no effort to conceal his anger. "Didn't I tell you not to play that music when I'm home?" he demanded. "Can't you do one single thing I ask?!"

Maggie stared at him open-mouthed, and though Sonny felt guilty for taking his mood out on her, he was too worked up to apologize yet.

"Turn it off!" he said impatiently, gesturing at the stereo. The song was grating on his nerves like a buzzsaw, and he knew his whole evening was completely ruined. He would spend it hurting like hell.

Maggie got a stubborn look on her young face, but she obeyed, and when there was once again silence in the room, Sonny grated out "Thanks," and started to turn away and go upstairs to change clothes.

Maggie froze him in his tracks by resentfully saying, "Well, it's not my album, Daddy. I found it down here when I was looking for something else. I don't know where it came from . . . do you?"

Sonny gritted his teeth, wishing to hell he'd remembered to ditch the album when things had blown up with Lissa.

"Well?" Maggie said, getting to her feet and facing him in almost a challenging way. "Who bought that album, Daddy? Somehow I don't think it was Mrs. Mullins. She goes more for stuff like Liberace."

Sonny took a breath, about to tell his daughter to mind her own business. Then he hesitated. He'd been taking his bad moods out on her more than she deserved lately, and it was time he stopped doing that.

"I bought it, Maggie," he said shortly, and as he turned away and started walking to the door, he added before Maggie could ask anything, "and I have no intention of telling you when or why, so drop it, okay?"

Maggie eyed his back speculatively. "Sure, Daddy," she finally said, then she quickly grabbed up the album cover and followed him. "But if you don't want it anymore, can I have it now?" she asked innocently. "I don't have this one, and I like the picture of Danny on this cover better than I do on their other albums."

Sonny stopped short and jerked his head around, frowning as he stared down at the cover in Maggie's hand. He wouldn't let his eyes rest on Lissa as the Vixen. Instead he concentrated on the dark-haired leader of the group, and was unable to stop himself from asking about him.

"Danny? This one? Let me see that."

Maggie handed the cover to him and as Sonny grimly studied Lissa's handsome lover, he felt his anger rising again.

"Danny's the leader of the Freaky Foursome," Maggie willingly explained. "Isn't he gorgeous? You can't really see the resemblance between him and Lissa when she's in makeup and costume like this . . . ," she pointed at Lissa on the cover, ". . . but . . ."

She realized something was wrong before she glanced up at her father's face and went abruptly silent.

Sonny was afraid to his soul that he hadn't heard Maggie correctly, or that if he had, he had drawn the wrong conclusion from her words.

"Why . . . ," he started to say, but his voice came out sounding so strained that he paused to clear his throat. "Why," he then repeated, "should there be a resemblance between this Danny and Lissa?"

Maggie was puzzled. Didn't her Dad know? But then she remembered that she'd found out Danny and Lissa were brother and sister from Lissa, and she was afraid her Dad would find out she'd talked to Lissa against his orders. After thinking quickly, however, she realized her Dad didn't have to know she'd talked to Lissa. Maggie could pretend she'd read it on the cover of an album or heard it somewhere.

"Because they're brother and sister, of course," she said innocently. "Can't you tell?"

Sonny closed his eyes, afraid to give in to the sudden intense joy suffusing him. Of course there was a resemblance between Danny and Lissa now that he thought about it! Why had he been so blind?

His eyes came open abruptly as a sudden fear hit him that it might not have been Danny who'd answered the phone that morning he'd called Lissa so early. "Does Danny ever stay with Lissa, Maggie?" he demanded.

Maggie didn't dare lie to her father when he was in this mood, even though being honest on this point was chancy.

"Sure . . . when he's in town," she said casually.

"Oh, my God!" Sonny felt sick over the way he'd jumped to conclusions.

Maggie was now torn between her curiosity over what was going on with her father and her feeling that she'd better get while the getting was good . . . before he found out she'd deliberately disobeyed one of his direct orders and been in contact with Lissa.

"Listen, Daddy, I've got to go do some homework," she said as she sidled around him and started for the stairs. "Call me when dinner's ready, okay?"

Sonny didn't even hear her, and Maggie quickly headed for the safety of her room, where instead of doing homework, she perched on her bed and wracked her brain trying to figure out why her father was acting so strange!

The black Ferrari was parked in Lissa's driveway and Sonny scowled at it. Though he knew most of what had happened was his own fault, he was furious that he'd wasted so much time and had to bear so much pain because of what Danny had implied on the phone that morning over a week ago.

Sonny rang the doorbell impatiently, expecting Lissa to open it. He was therefore taken aback when a young woman he'd never seen before opened the door instead.

"Yes?" Darla said, thinking the man outside was certainly handsome and well dressed for a door-to-door salesman . . . if that was what he was.

"Is Lissa home?" Sonny asked crisply. "I'd like to speak to her."

Darla stared at him and began to put two and two together. From Lissa's description of Sonny Strotherton, this had to be him.

"That depends," she said thoughtfully. "Are you Sonny Strotherton?"

Sonny showed his surprise. "Yes, I am. Why?"

"Because if you are and you're here to break Lissa's heart again, she's not home to you," Darla said bluntly.

It was Sonny's turn to stare now, but after a moment, he began to smile. "Well, I'm glad to know Lissa's got a protector," he said with humor, "but breaking Lissa's heart is the last thing I have in mind."

Darla hesitated for another moment, studying Sonny's handsome smiling face intently, before she made up her mind.

"Okay," she said, stepping back to let Sonny in the house. "She's in her father's study . . . studying, naturally. That's all she ever does these days." Her voice imparted a faintly accusing note to the last sentence.

173

Sonny ignored it and gave Darla a stunning smile as he stepped past her and headed for the study.

As he approached the closed study door, Jay, dressed in his white karate outfit, came down the hall from the direction of the kitchen and stopped short at seeing Sonny.

"Well . . . hello . . . ?" Jay said curiously.

Sonny didn't bat an eye. At this point, Elvis Presley could have risen from the grave and confronted him in Lissa's hallway, and Sonny would have walked right past him.

"Hello," he responded with a nod, and without pausing, he opened the study door and disappeared inside, shutting the door firmly behind him.

CHAPTER FIFTEEN

Elizabeth was curled up on the leather sofa with her dark head bent over a textbook. She was concentrating so intensely that she didn't hear Sonny come into the room, and he stood silently for a moment drinking in the sight of her.

Then Elizabeth sensed his presence and looked up. Sonny saw her eyes widen and her lovely skin pale with the shock of seeing him there, and, in a flash, he was across the room, kneeling in front of her.

Elizabeth drew back and stared at him as though she'd never seen him before.

"Don't look at me like that, Lissa," Sonny pleaded softly. He reached and pulled the book she held from her resisting fingers, then took her hands in his own. "We've got to clear things up between us."

Elizabeth continued to stare at him, her gaze turning hostile. Though her heart was beating with excitement at seeing Sonny again and having him touch her, her mind was simmering with anger.

"I tried that," she said flatly. "You wouldn't let me explain."

Sonny nodded. "Because I thought another man had won you, Lissa. I thought you were sleeping with him and had chosen him over me."

That was the last thing Elizabeth had expected him to say, and she couldn't hide her shock.

Sonny began to explain, speaking quickly. "I've always thought there was another man in the picture, Lissa, and that's why you were reluctant to get involved with me. But I thought we had so much going for us, I could beat him out eventually. Then, the evening I got back from Florida, I called here for hours, and you didn't answer. It bothered me, but I didn't go around the bend until I called here very early the next morning, and Danny answered the phone . . . only I didn't know it was Danny, or that he was your brother. And since it was obvious he'd just woken up, and he implied some things that led me to believe he and you were . . ."

Sonny paused, unable to put into words what he'd thought. His expression pained, he shrugged and added, *"Then,* I went around the bend. I thought you'd made your choice in his favor, and I was devastated."

Elizabeth's head was whirling, and her expression showed her complete incredulity. "You mean it wasn't because you found out that I was the Vixen that you shut me out?"

Sonny shook his head and took a deep breath. "I admit, that was a shock as well, and I was furious that you'd been keeping something like that a secret from me, but I was even more furious at seeing you up there on that stage with the man I thought you'd chosen over me. Later, when I calmed down, I realized my attitude about the Vixen was the reason you didn't tell me. That it was my own fault you'd kept it from me. But there was still Danny between us, you see, and I couldn't get around him."

Elizabeth was too dazed to comment for a moment. She still couldn't completely accept the truth. "But you looked so furious when you left the auditorium," she finally said.

"I was," Sonny agreed. "I saw you and Danny up on that stage together, and it nearly killed me. Anger was better than dealing with all that pain."

"But I sang you that special song to tell you how I felt," Lissa said, torn between her still-simmering resentment toward Sonny over the pain he'd caused her and a burgeoning sympathy for the pain he'd endured.

Sonny lifted his shoulders in a gesture of futility. "When I realized who you were, that song and the way you sang it went right out of my head, Lissa. I was irrational, I guess. I couldn't think straight and sort it all out."

Elizabeth closed her eyes and shook her head in disbelief, then opened them again and glared at Sonny.

"But Sonny, I told you in the beginning there wasn't another man in my life!"

Sonny grimaced and shook his head. "You weren't very convincing, Lissa. And another man was the only reason I could come up with that you wanted to ignore what was happening between you and me."

Lissa knew she hadn't been convincing that night she'd told Sonny there wasn't anyone else in her life, but she was still angry and didn't want to let him off the hook.

"And the night we first met at the charity concert, Danny mentioned during his introduction that he came from a local medical family, and that was why we were doing the benefit concert. Didn't you put two and two together when you learned I was the Vixen?"

"He did?" Sonny looked and felt blank. "I didn't hear him," he said. "I guess I just wasn't listening. I was too upset about Maggie's infatuation with you and the group."

That remark crystallized Elizabeth's anger at him. "Yes, I could tell what you thought of me," she said bitterly, "and it became even clearer when you came back to my dressing room after the show in New York."

Sonny didn't try to deny it, nor did he hide his look of regret. "I know. I thought you were a tramp, and I was ashamed of myself for being attracted to such a woman. I didn't understand it. But that song you sang at the first concert . . . the special one—'You're the Only Man for Me.' That song got to me, Lissa. I went out and bought the damned album and sneaked around like a kid to listen to it. And when you sang it again at the club, I came back to see you to try to understand what the hell was going on with me more than anything else. Then, when you kissed me—"

"It's the fact that you thought I was a tramp from the beginning that bothers me, Sonny," she broke in coldly. "And that you thought you were too good to be attracted to someone you were judging unfairly anyway."

Sonny nodded. "I don't blame you for being upset with me, Lissa. I was a prejudiced snob. All I can do is ask your forgiveness and try not to be such a jerk in the future."

Elizabeth hesitated. His willingness to apologize, and to try to do better began to take the steam out of her anger with him. Then, she remembered that she hadn't helped matters with the performance she'd put on in her dressing room the night he'd kissed her for the first time, and her anger melted a little more.

"I deliberately played on your prejudice against the type of woman you thought I was in my dressing room in New York that time, Sonny," she admitted, her tone more reasonable.

Sonny was puzzled. "Well, I admit I was wrong to judge you without knowing you," he said, "but why did you behave so out of character and try to make me think you were going to sleep with someone for giving you a job?"

Lissa sighed and shook her head. "Because I sensed it would get rid of you, and I was afraid of you."

Sonny felt astonished. "Afraid of me? *Why*, for God's sake?"

Elizabeth gave him a level look. "Because you were a doctor, Sonny . . . and more important, you were a doctor who practiced in Boston who had exactly the sort of prejudice against rock singers that worried me. That's what the makeup and clothes were all about, Sonny. I didn't want the medical community here in Boston to find out I was playing the role of the Vixen temporarily. I was afraid they would never take me seriously, and my career as a doctor would be damaged for completely spurious reasons."

Sonny hung his head in an expression of shame and disbelief for a moment, before he raised it again and shook it, staring at Lissa with helpless regret.

Slowly, Elizabeth's anger drained away completely. She began to accept that Sonny really had learned his lesson and that he was sincerely sorry for the misunderstandings his prejudice had caused between them.

"Sonny . . . ," she began tentatively.

"Yes?" he responded, gazing at her with tender love and dawning hope in his eyes.

His look made Elizabeth smile. "Aren't you uncomfortable down there on your knees? Why don't you come sit beside me?"

Sonny looked even more hopeful. "I have a better idea," he said as he stood up without letting go of Elizabeth's hands. "Why don't you come up here with me?"

Gently, he tugged at her hands, and his heart surged as she allowed him to pull her to her feet and stood gazing at him as though she were waiting for something.

"Lissa . . . ," he said softly. "I love you completely. Please say you forgive me and give me another chance."

Lissa hesitated. "What if I have to fill in for Darla again someday?" she asked quietly. "Will that bother you? Can you love me as the Vixen, too?"

Sonny held her gaze steadily, a small smile on his lips. "I wanted the Vixen before I wanted Lissa Farrell," he replied. "Now, if I can have both of you, I'll be the happiest man alive."

Elizabeth believed him, and she began to feel as though a heavy weight were slipping off her shoulders, leaving her free to enjoy life to the fullest . . . to love Sonny the way she'd always wanted to love him.

"Then what are you waiting for?" she asked softly. "Both of us are here for the taking."

Staring down into her eyes, Sonny whispered, "Not a thing."

And he bent to her mouth, kissing her with reverential sweetness at first, until Lissa circled his neck with her arms and leaned into him. Then, the fire that had been simmering inside him for so long burst into flame and the kiss took on an entirely different character.

Elizabeth met his kiss with as much urgency as he gave it, until both of them knew they couldn't go on like this until they had complete privacy. Then they simply held on to one another, very tightly, for a few long, frustratingly satisfying moments.

Finally, Elizabeth drew back and said shakily, "Come on. I guess I'd better introduce you to the rest of my household."

Sonny gave her a speaking look. "Can we be alone together later? I still feel petrified when I think of how close I came to losing you . . . and we've waited long enough, don't you think?"

Elizabeth searched his face with her eyes, suddenly fearing her own capacity to satisfy him. "I hope I don't disappoint you, Sonny," she said softly. "I'm not at all experienced."

"I'd begun to guess that." He smiled at her tenderly. "But don't worry about disappointing me, darling. It won't happen."

He enjoyed Elizabeth's look of relief and anticipation enormously, then his curiosity got the better of him. "Why aren't you experienced, Lissa?" he asked. "Have you never been in love before?" He hoped she hadn't. He wanted to be everything to her.

"No, I've never been in love until now," Lissa said, and received a stunning look of love for her confession. "But it wasn't only that. I'm a doctor's daughter, remember? By the age of twelve, I knew every technical detail about sex there is and I didn't need to experiment to find out what it was all about. It held no mysteries for me . . . at least, no *intellectual* mysteries." She gazed at him with her heart in her eyes, and added, very softly, "It wasn't until I met you that I began to understand what sex is really all about."

Sonny returned her look, feeling joyous and yet humble . . . eager and yet a little scared of the responsibility of introducing Lissa to her own womanhood. He hoped it didn't turn out that he was the one who disappointed her.

"Then I hope I don't disappoint you either," he said, his voice husky.

Elizabeth smiled at him, and the smile was sweetly sensual. "I'm not in the least worried about that," she assured him softly. "If your foreplay is any indication, I can't wait for the rest of the experience."

Sonny suddenly grinned, and his eyes began to glow with heated anticipation. "I can't either," he said, "so let's get married as soon as possible."

A knock on the door prevented Elizabeth from answering, and Sonny groaned and closed his eyes.

"Come in," Elizabeth called, laughter in her voice.

Darla stuck her head in the door. "Dinner's ready," she said with a cheerful lack of repentance over what she'd interrupted. "Are you two hungry?"

In a dryly resigned tone, and perfectly straight-faced, Sonny answered for both of them. "I think I can safely say we're both starved."

Later that night, in a suite Sonny rented in Boston's best hotel, Elizabeth came out of the bathroom dressed in her best peignoir, and found Sonny waiting as eagerly for her as she could wish for. She wasn't the least nervous, and she came into his arms as naturally as though they were already married, though the wedding wouldn't be held until the following Saturday.

She wrapped her arms around his neck and smiled her sweetest smile. "I think my brother was a little shocked when you carried me away with you," she teased, "though I guess it helped when you told him you were going to make an honest woman of me next week."

Though Sonny could understand how any brother might feel under the circumstances, his grin was unrepentant. Despite Danny's explanation of why he'd behaved as he had on the phone with Sonny, Sonny had rather enjoyed paying Danny Farrell back for that early-morning conversation they'd had which had resulted in one of the worst weeks in Sonny's life.

"I can see you aren't interested in Danny's brotherly feelings," Elizabeth said with mock soberness.

"Not in the least," Sonny agreed. "The only feelings I'm interested in right now are yours and mine." And he ran his hands up the silk of Elizabeth's gown suggestively, while his eyes began to take on a glow Elizabeth recognized and which excited her into a breathless state.

"I feel the same," she murmured, moving closer to him. "So take me to bed, Dr. Strotherton. I've read all the texts on sex, and now I'm ready for some hands-on experimentation."

"You really are a Vixen underneath that ladylike exterior, aren't you?" Sonny said with a great deal of satisfaction. "And I'll be more than happy to complete your education."

Elizabeth was amazed when Sonny bent and picked her up in his arms to carry her to the bed.

"That wasn't in the textbooks," she said with surprised approval after he kissed her, then placed her on the bed and straightened to remove his clothes.

"I have a lot of things to teach you they don't put in books." Sonny grinned as he joined her under the covers.

"Oh, I *hope* so," Elizabeth said fervently as she came into his arms and snuggled against him. "Those illustrations were so . . . so . . ."

"Technical?" Sonny teased, caressing her with his smile and his look as surely as he had begun to with his hands.

"And emotionally sterile," Elizabeth agreed breathlessly, lifting her mouth for a kiss.

Sonny kissed her in a way intended to erase any notion she might still have that making love had anything to do with technical sex, and in the process reduced Elizabeth to a state of trembling anticipation.

"Show me more," she whispered huskily, when Sonny at last let her breathe again.

"With pleasure," he murmured huskily, and moved his mouth to the base of her throat before beginning to trace an erotic path from there to the curve of her breast above the nightgown she wore.

As he nuzzled her flesh in a tantalizing way, Elizabeth cupped the back of his neck with her hand, aiding his exploration.

"Wouldn't this work better if I didn't have this gown on?" she finally suggested, her voice trembling slightly.

Sonny raised his head, and his smile and the gleam of blue fire in his eyes were as exciting to Elizabeth as his touch.

"That's another thing the textbooks don't tell you," he said in a low, erotically caressing tone. "There's an art to each stage along the road to where we want to go."

"Then I'll be quiet and learn, while you demonstrate," Elizabeth said shakily.

Sonny shook his head. "I don't want you to be quiet," he said, his voice thickening as he watched Lissa's reaction to the rubbing of his thumb near the tip of her breast. "And I don't want merely to demonstrate. I want you participating in everything that happens between us from beginning to end."

Elizabeth's eyes began to cloud with passion, and her willing smile grew sensually inviting. "Oh . . . well, in that case . . . ," she whispered from deep in her throat. Pressing on the back of his neck, she raised herself slightly to meet his mouth, kissing him as uninhibitedly as though they'd been making love for years.

Sometime later, they passed the point where Sonny demonstrated the fine art of removing her gown, and he was poised above her, his eyes glistening with a mixture of passion and concern.

"This may hurt a bit at first," he said, his voice grating thickly with the effort he was making to hold on to his control.

"No, darling . . . ," Elizabeth gasped. "I want you. Do it, Sonny . . . please . . . now . . ." And her next gasp was one of pain as Sonny obliged, but the pain was quickly replaced by pleasure.

"Darling, I'm sorry," Sonny said shakenly, his body and mind in severe conflict.

"Don't be," Elizabeth said shakily. "Just make love to me."

And slowly, with tender gentleness at first, they made love until Elizabeth had completely forgotten the hurt of the initial invasion and was again caught up in the joy of his loving.

Sonny reacted to her vibrant response by gradually loosening the tight rein he was holding on himself, and as the power of his lovemaking increased, Elizabeth's senses began to reel. She gave an inarticulate little cry of surprise and pleasure as she felt herself going completely over the edge of control and plunging into the shuddering bliss of sheer ecstasy, and she held Sonny tightly against her as she felt him join her in a shuddering release of his own.

Later, as their breathing eased and they held one another in a loose embrace of contented exhaustion, Elizabeth smiled and asked drowsily, "Was it worth the wait?"

Sonny gave a tired chuckle. "More than worth it," he acknowledged.

"I'm glad," Elizabeth said contentedly.

He turned his head on the pillow to look at her lovingly. "And what about you?" he teased. "Are you pleased with the difference in mere illustrations and the reality of love?"

Elizabeth pretended to ponder the matter, but when she sensed Sonny's very real concern over her delay in answering, she relented. "Well, I have to admit . . . for a moment there, I was ready to go back to the books. But then you showed me what a mistake that would be."

The look of relief on Sonny's face brought a soft chuckle from her and she hugged him close. "Oh, Sonny, you didn't really need to ask, did you?" she said lovingly. "You felt what happened to me."

"Yes, I did and I shared the ecstasy," he answered. "But the experiment isn't over yet, my love. Not by a long shot."

Elizabeth snuggled closer and sighed her contentment. "That's the beauty of knowledge, isn't it?" she teased. "You never get to the end of the learning process."

"God, I hope not," Sonny vowed emphatically and found her mouth to begin taking the second tiny step on a journey he knew would take them the rest of their lives to complete and would give them an endless source of contentment and joy as they made their way down the road.

Maggie, naturally, was in seventh heaven at the wedding. The only way she could have been happier was if her friends could have known that Lissa had once been the Vixen and could have attended the wedding so that Maggie could introduce all of them to the Foursome as well as her new stepmother. She was pacified, however, because there was no rule against her disclosing Lissa's (and therefore Maggie's) family connection with the Freaky Foursome, and Maggie's popularity at school was soaring as a result.

Among the wedding gifts was a block of stock in a new medical technology firm from Jay, a complete new Vixen costume and makeup kit from Darla (for when the honeymoon was over, she said blandly) and the rights to the song, "You're the Only Man for Me," from Danny.

Because neither of them wanted to waste time traveling, they went to a friend's cottage on Cape Cod for their honeymoon.

That evening, a mild storm blew in, and as Sonny and Elizabeth sat in snug safety in front of a blazing fire, drinking wine and listening to the wind howling around the cottage, neither could stop smiling between kisses.

Suddenly, Elizabeth remembered something and made Sonny release her, which he did with a great deal of reluctance.

"Where are you going?" he complained as she jumped up from the sofa and raced to the bedroom.

"You'll see," she called out as she rummaged in the bottom of her suitcase and withdrew a record album. A moment later the record was on the turntable and the strains of Ravel's *Bolero* wafted through the living room of the cottage.

Elizabeth stood beside the stereo in her new white peignoir and grinned at Sonny's confused expression. "I lied when I said I didn't think it aided romance," she explained happily. "I do."

Sonny gave her a chiding look as he got to his feet. "Maybe it does," he said as he headed for the bedroom, "but I know something that works even better."

Now Elizabeth looked confused as Sonny came out a moment later with a record in his hands.

"What's that?" she asked curiously.

"You'll see," Sonny said mysteriously as he stopped the stereo, removed the record Elizabeth had put on it, and substituted his own. He then programmed the stereo so that it would play only one of the selections on the album and turned to Elizabeth, holding his arms out to her.

She was still looking puzzled as she accepted the invitation. Her expression cleared abruptly and she began smiling as the introduction to "You're the Only Man for Me" began.

"That's *our* song," Sonny murmured as he rested his cheek against Elizabeth's hair and started to move slowly to the music. "Nobody else's."

"Literally," Elizabeth agreed happily, and began to sing softly along with herself into Sonny's ear, putting every bit of love she felt for him into her voice.

When the song was finishing, Sonny's mouth captured the last word on Elizabeth's lips, and while he was kissing her, he began to back her to their former position in front of the fireplace. He lifted her and placed her among the cushions on the floor, and when he was beside her, he cupped her face in his hand and stared down at her with such an erotically possessive gleam in his blue eyes that Elizabeth shivered in response.

"Are we going to make love here?" she whispered.

Sonny smiled slightly. "Are you comfortable?" he whispered back, and when she nodded, he said, "Then yes . . . we're going to make love for the first time as man and wife right here. I want to start off our married love the way I intend it to go on . . . as a waking fantasy, with no holds barred, no inhibitions to get in the way. The Vixen taught me that."

Elizabeth opened her eyes wide. "But you never made love to the Vixen, Sonny," she pointed out.

Sonny's smile was malely wicked. "Didn't I?" And when Elizabeth looked puzzled, he explained. "One kiss, and the Vixen invaded my dreams. I made fierce love to her almost every night after that kiss, Lissa. And now that I've got her in my arms for real, and you as well, I'm going to start living some of those dreams . . . if you have no objections?"

The look in Elizabeth's eyes answered for her so vividly that Sonny gave a rasping groan and seized her mouth in a fervid kiss that sparked off exactly the sort of fierce lovemaking he'd dreamed about with the Vixen.

Far from objecting, Elizabeth, with joyous abandon, matched his every searching, demanding touch and kiss. The dancing flames in the grate and the moaning wind outside the cabin were no more elemental than the two nude figures hungrily exploring the limits of their passion for one another. The security of mutual love and respect gave each of them the courage to abandon caution and let the wild, reckless side of their natures come to the surface and flow freely with life and vigor.

And when it was over, Sonny knew with utter certainty that he'd found every man's dream—a complete woman, possessed of every grace and attribute of her gender, as well as a good many of those he admired in his own.

And Elizabeth knew she was the luckiest woman in the world to have found a man who could appreciate her for who she was, as well as draw out things in her she hadn't known were there and was happily joyous to find.

EPILOGUE

Dr. Elizabeth Strotherton rose eagerly from her chair in her office next door to Sonny's and greeted the first youthful patient of many she would have as a private physician.

"Hello, there," she said cheerfully to the twelve-year-old girl who was here for a school physical and was at the moment staring at a large, colorful picture of a musical group which was hanging on the wall behind Elizabeth's desk.

Elizabeth smiled happily over the girl's interest, and she was filled with relief that she no longer had to hide her past. Now that she was a full-fledged doctor and had Sonny's emotional support, the rest of the medical community's approval or lack of it meant little to her. She even enjoyed filling in for Darla occasionally these days.

The girl's mother frowned when her daughter didn't answer Elizabeth's greeting right away, but instead, continued staring at the poster.

"Sally, where are your manners?" the woman said chidingly. "Say hello to the doctor."

The girl came out of her absorption with the poster and transferred her gaze to Elizabeth, staring at her with wide-eyed awe.

"Were you really once the Vixen?" she asked breathlessly.

Elizabeth smiled and was about to answer when the mother broke in.

"I'm sorry, Dr. Strotherton, but Sally's fascinated by that group. Normally, I wouldn't be happy about it, but she's always been afraid of doctors and it was like pulling teeth to get her to one. But when she heard about you . . ." The mother smiled, shrugged and held out her hands as though to say, "What can you do with children this age?"

Elizabeth chuckled and came to put her arm around the girl's shoulders.

"Yes, I was once the Vixen, Sally. Why don't you come in here to the examining room, and I'll tell you all about it. And if you like, when this examination is over," she added warmly as the girl climbed up on the examining couch, "I'll give you an autographed poster of the Freaky Foursome that you can hang on your own wall at home."

"If I *like?*" Sally said with happy incredulity. "Gosh, Vixen, I'd do anything to get an autographed picture of the Foursome!"

"You don't have to do anything," Elizabeth said as she put her stethoscope in her ears. "Just sit still while I find out if you're as healthy as you look."

Around noon, Sonny came to his wife's door and leaned against the jamb, watching her with admiration and love in his eyes as she finished marking a chart.

"Ready for lunch, Dr. Strotherton?" he asked when she finally glanced up and noticed him.

"Am I ever!" she said happily as she jumped up from her chair and started taking off her white coat. "I can't wait to tell you how my morning went. Maggie was right. The kids are so crazy about the Foursome posters, I think they'd let me take out their tonsils twice just to get their hands on one."

Sonny grinned as he came and took Elizabeth into his arms and planted a kiss on her upturned lips. "I think they're probably more impressed with the Vixen than the Foursome," he teased warmly, adoring her with his eyes. "But as for me, I have one complaint about that notorious tramp."

Elizabeth looked at him askance. "If you do, it isn't apparent," she said skeptically. "You look disgustingly happy."

"So I am, so I am," Sonny agreed. "But I'll be even happier when the Vixen stops relapsing occasionally into wearing skimpy camisoles and miniskirts and starts buying maternity smocks."

Elizabeth, who was in possession of some knowledge that Sonny did not yet have, smiled secretly. "Well," she said lightly as she drew Sonny out the door of her office, "why don't you reserve a cottage on Cape Cod for the long weekend that's coming up and direct your considerable charms in my direction. You just might be able to persuade me to see things your way."

Sonny's eyes lit up with anticipation and he was unusually solicitous of Elizabeth as he walked her to their car and helped her inside it.

When he was settled beside her, Elizabeth gave him a puzzled look.

"Why are you being so blatantly gentlemanly?" she asked. "I'm not made of glass, you know."

Sonny smiled a secret smile of his own, and Elizabeth's eyes widened as she realized he had guessed her secret.

"Sonny Strotherton!" she said crossly. "How long have you known, and why haven't you said anything?"

Sonny's expression was serene as he reached over and gave her a loving pat on the knee.

"I'm a doctor, too, remember, Mrs. Strotherton?" he said smugly. "As well as a husband. The doctor in me knew almost immediately, but the husband was waiting for his wife to give him the glad news."

Elizabeth couldn't stay cross with him, and she began to chuckle. "Does this mean we don't get the weekend at Cape Cod?" she teased.

Now, it was Sonny's turn to chuckle and as he did, he glanced at Elizabeth with a wicked twinkle in his eyes.

"Only an idiot would give up a weekend with the Vixen," he said blandly, "and I've always considered myself pretty smart."

Elizabeth gave him one of her sweetest smiles. "Me, too," she agreed with his self-evaluation. "Now, let's get to the restaurant, Sonny. I'm ready to start eating for two . . . or more," she added slyly.

When Sonny looked at her with a startled expression on his face, she gave him an even sweeter smile.

"Vixens usually don't have single births, Doctor. Didn't you take any zoology courses in college?"

And as Sonny's startlement turned to dismay, Elizabeth burst out laughing and gave him a hug and a kiss to ease the blow. She would wait until their weekend on Cape Cod to tell him she'd deceived him once again.